ONE
FOR THE DEVIL

Also by Etienne Leroux

Seven Days at the Silbersteins

ONE
FOR THE DEVIL

Etienne Leroux

Translated from Afrikaans
by Charles Eglington

~~~~~~~~~~~~~~~~~~~~~~~~~~~~~~~~

Houghton Mifflin Company Boston • 1968

First Printing   c

25,633

Dedicated to John Kannemeyer

"Therefore the tragic figure of our time is perhaps he who takes guilt upon himself to make valid for ourselves our hate or sorrow," said Dr. Johns.

(In a Foundation like Welgevonden all characters are imaginary and all events probable. Everyone who recognizes himself in any of the characters belongs on Welgevonden.)

CONTENTS

Ubi? 1

Quid? 7

Cur? 13

Quis? 19

Quibus Auxiliis? 159

Quomodo? 171

Quando? 199

UBI?

UBI? · The lawn stretched between clumps of trees and shrubs that appeared here and there like islands: an artificial green sea on which its creator wandered with his wife, the "slim" Mrs. Silberstein, and his setter. It was a beautiful, restless animal, nourished on concentrates and cod liver oil to black and white Spanish pride — skin soft as silk, eyes dark and moistly shining, free from ophthalmia, ears flapping and tail waving: a useless end-product that lent grace to an aimless stroll. Sometimes it appeared against the hillside, a patch of light on the green; then it vanished into the darkness of a branch, a tree stump, a shadow.

Seen from that corner of the estate, Welgevonden was still in its renaissance and the Silbersteins could have been Medicis, the two of them, if one could imagine them cloaked, if one could change the language they spoke and if, at that moment, there had not been a fault in her voice as she called "Fido!"

Eighteen years past one's full flowering brought a toughness of sinews where formerly there had been suppleness and slimness; robbed the voice of its music and, at a certain pitch, caused flexibility to fail, so that there was a crack in the call "Fido! Fido!" What had once been, perhaps, an interesting banality became simply commonplace because, alas, the Medicis have long been dead.

And for him, too, eighteen years in which to become stocky; eighteen years to hunch those broad shoulders, to bleach the blue of the eyes, to deprive rough, youthful masculinity of its youthfulness and begin gnawing already at masculinity itself, so that perhaps one day there would remain only roughness to remind one — of what, exactly? A roughness in his voice, therefore, as he added it to hers, and his "Fido! Fido!" had the desired effect, since the dog now appeared on the crest of the hill, sharply outlined against the horizon.

They hesitated for a moment and looked with admiration tempered by wistfulness at the silhouette: the pointing attitude, nose raised, tail motionless; restrained concentration which, in the silence before movement, was charged with more movement than movement itself, a state of tension just this side of completion that left something to the imagination — a picture of Timomachus that surprised one in the transient moment. And then, suddenly, the forepaw was raised and the animal stiffened into the catatonic posture characteristic of its breed.

"What would he be seeing?" asked Jock Silberstein.

"Are there still partridges?" said "slim" Mrs. Silberstein.

Hand in hand they hurried up the hillside, past the dog, and then looked somewhat myopically back and forth across the lawn. Years ago they would not have been as breathless as they were now and there would have been something brisk in their movements. They looked up: in the distance a thousand diamonds glittered in the air as the leaves of poplar trees moved. Then they caught sight of the plastic swan, inflated, dun colored, blown by the wind from the fountain, over shrubs, through the hollows, to a point close by exactly in the middle of the lawn; neatly in position, swollen and discolored, its arched neck still endlessly on the move.

"Just imagine," said "slim" Mrs. Silberstein.

"I was always under the impression that they went by *scent*," said Jock Silberstein.

It was something they could tell their friends. "Slim" Mrs. Silberstein stroked the dog, which at once relaxed, nosed her and then dashed off in the direction of the fountain. It was something they would always remember: an anecdote that would be often aired about the setter and the plastic swan; that would remain with them always, a piece of *kitsch* on the mantelshelf of their memories.

At the foot of the Welgevonden mountain the trout lake was fed by small streams that began somewhere among the peaks and wet heather. To prevent erosion, Jock Silberstein many years ago had twenty Italian prisoners of war build retaining walls with overflows in the middle, to allow so many cusecs to flow off after the dams, which were to keep back the sludge, became full. This was during the Second World War and these men had had to be kept occupied, preferably in some artistic way. The result of months of activity reflected their state of mind: each cement retaining wall had been fashioned on the outside in the form of a tragic mask, with the overflows sculpted in the shape of dripping mouths. This left the impression of a series of huge gargoyle waterspouts, all down the mountainside to the lake. Thereafter the same motif had been repeated on the overflows, from where a single stream tumbled down the hill, across the Welgevonden lawns to the fountain. The fountain, itself almost a lake, was smothered under water lilies, surrounded by marble statues and populated by plastic swans. It served in reality as a camouflaged reservoir for all the water installations connected with the farm's activities, but it had always been the policy at Welgevonden to conceal the functional behind an aesthetic facade.

With the passage of time, moss had covered the masks and given them a many-colored patina, so that they gave the impression of having been fashioned centuries ago — like statues that one would expect to come across against the slopes of Mediterranean mountains. Mostly the little rippling streams flowed peacefully, and then the masks dribbled clear, red, mountain water; but when it had just rained, as now, each one spurted a froth-laden red stream into the air.

During the day the sun gleamed on the masks and they shivered in hazy mirages; at dusk they grimaced somberly and roused in one feelings of approaching doom; at night one was aware of the masks, although they could not be seen. With the years they had become much weathered and had not been repaired: here a nose had been broken off, there was a harelip through which the water seeped. But there were so many buildings and coppices on Welgevonden that it was sometimes days or months before one noticed the masks for the first time. After that, one could not forget them.

On this sunny afternoon after the rain a setter in a crazy mood was dashing to and fro across the grass. In the distance his master and mistress could be seen. He had just pointed out to them a plastic swan that had been blown from the fountain. Now he reached the fountain itself and something caught his attention.

QUID?

QUID? · "There's something at the
fountain," said Jock Silberstein when the
dog became motionless for the second time.
"Slim" Mrs. Silberstein raised her hand to her
mouth. "The fountain . . ." she said and turned her
face toward the maze of buildings far below, as if in the laby-
rinths of Welgevonden she would find assurance.

"It's most likely a plastic swan," said Jock Silberstein, un-
easy with the knowledge that patterns repeat themselves, that
each event tends to recur in its own image.

For a moment they remained thus, outwardly still: the tableau of a dog in a graceful, suggestive line pointing to the invisible something in the fountain, and of an intermediary in
the form of a divided man with his arms stretched out on
either side, to connect the tense dog with an evasive woman.
The tension reached a climax, collapsed and disintegrated in
the leisurely movement of the woman who moved away and
down, to the rounded gables, the flaming walls, the innumerable windows and the complex courtyards that offered protection against a dangerous simplicity. The wind played lightly
with her modish dress, it dissolved the severity of *haute
couture* to the frivolity of a Botticelli gown, it creased and
waved around her in graceful flight. Middle-aged Mrs. Silberstein became more youthful with increasing distance; she became attenuated by distance to the slim Mrs. Silberstein of
eighteen years ago.

"It's a plastic swan," repeated Jock Silberstein and then
turned to the dog which remained motionless in a waiting
position. Before him the fountain moved in a continuous

eddy as the water under the water-lily leaves poured away perpetually through cement pipes at the bottom. The swan's doubles — white, dun gray and inflated — bobbed around directionlessly. In the distance the waters spurted, the masks stuck out their red tongues, the sun gleamed against the grotesque faces. Jock pushed his hat back and wiped the sweat from his forehead. He stared across the estate: the factory in the distance, the house there below, the moving speck that must be his wife. Then he stroked the dog which by its own compulsion was still faithfully immobile.

"What is it, Fido? What's up, old man?"

His attention was attracted to something that was drifting on the stream toward the fountain: something that moved shapelessly through the water, that dipped and vanished, and then appeared among the swans, imitating their directionlessness, and then suddenly got caught in a piece of flotsam and, slowly, began to move around and around, counterclockwise. Around and around it revolved, sometimes visible, sometimes unseen, around and around like a minute hand moving in the reverse direction. A grayish object — but what was it? And now that his master was also aware of it, the dog relaxed, as if its part in the game were complete.

In the meantime Jock Silberstein had removed his hat and held it in front of his eyes to shade them from the sun; he peered from the shadow of the brim and as his eyes became accustomed to the movement, adjusted themselves to the movement, the object became recognizable. Jock Silberstein's head moved around and around as he followed the rotation, with every completed revolution his horror grew, his emotions swung visibly from horror, shock, incredulity, realization, grief, back to horror. He was powerless with his head following all the motions and gradually his movements became autonomous. He stood there like a big doll with a built-in mechanism. And then tears began slowly to trickle from his eyes. His mouth opened and closed and he wept soundlessly, caught up in the never-ending circle. After a while he began involuntarily to make small sounds, like a mute trying to speak; later the sounds became louder but were still wordless and inhuman; eventually he gave himself over completely to his grief and stumbled into the water with a cry that cut through the midday air and vanished without echo.

CUR?

CUR? · He walked across the expanse of lawn with the dripping objects in his arms. His movements seemed to be purposeless; and his strength was superhuman as he simply walked on and on past the buildings, through the windows of which they looked at him, in the panes of which he saw himself. All impressions came simultaneously and incoherently. He stumbled on and suddenly saw all their images disintegrate in the various mirrors. They looked out at him from the mirrors . . . They looked at him through binoculars . . . The mirrors splintered in a thousand pieces and the images shattered with them. The windows were the viewfinders on their cameras, through which they peered. They aimed at one another and then the lens was directed at him. They had dissected one another and now they dissected him as he walked on purposelessly across the lawn with his burden.

Then he was alone again, a gigantic figure in the measureless landscape.

At a certain moment he appeared to have found his direction. He arrived at the factory and the cellars. He entered through the big gateway and descended, level after level below the ground, to the innermost sanctuary where the *finos* had been aged. Carefully, he laid the corpse on a table. Here were and had been all the things that encompassed his great love, where everything had come to an end and been reborn. Here was the entire significant, incomprehensible cycle. Here everything was present, lifeless and yet alive. He could no longer distinguish between beginning and end. He felt old, and like an old man could no longer come to a conclusion.

This is my whole life, all my achievements and all my disappointments. I can think no further and for the rest of my time on earth I shall be petrified at this point. What is true? What is not true? What has happened? Why did it all happen? Why does it end or begin here?

At a certain stage he walked to and fro in the cellar. The electric light burned from a single, naked globe. Outside, perhaps, dusk had already begun to fall. He walked to and fro and then he went and stood by the object on the table. He looked closely at the face, as if he had never seen it before. He fingered the hair, at times, and tried to arrange it, but it was wet and clammy and unmanageable. Small things attracted his attention: the shape of the nose, the lips, the eyebrows, two small marks on the throat, the tips of the fingers. A drop of blood had congealed on the skin. He looked at its color. Sometimes certain articles of the clothing caught his attention and he wondered where and when he had bought them. He recalled the time when he had given this and that as a little gift, and how the few moments of real pleasure had left a warm feeling deep inside him.

There was blood on the lips and between the teeth. A strong feeling of alarm overpowered him and he walked quickly away through the passages, outside, to the steam room where the copper pipes intertwined on the walls like serpents. He opened the steam cock and waited until the sound of steam eliminated all sound and then he began to bellow. It lasted longer than usual: he shouted the questions at the noisy silence, but received no answer and felt no release. This, too, had had to happen: that the room of confession should lose its healing power. When he went outside the sun had already set and a red glow played malignantly on the spurting masks against the mountain.

He walked slowly and resolutely back to the cellars, to the innermost chamber where the object lay on the table. To one side in a corner was a heavy club and he picked it up.

Precisely at sunset the sounds began, the noise of copper and earthenware being broken: the liberating destruction, the safeguard against evil in all its forms, the forgotten ritual of a Jew of Tripoli, the noise *sub magiae fugiendae praetextu*, the assault on death in oneself.

And outside the door, attracted by the noise, there listened Detective-Sergeant Demosthenes H. de Goede. He looked rather like Jacques Tati in his part as a postman. He was utterly incapable of formulating a single sentence.

"Pittttt-Pittttt . . ." he stammered. "Brrrrr . . . Psssst. Mmmmmmmm . . . ffffffft!"

QUIS?

QUIS? · Chapter One · The Interment ·· "The technical sequence of the
unraveling of the heptagonal problem is very
strict, according to Quintillus," Dr. Johns said to
Detective-Sergeant Demosthenes H. de Goede. "Who?
What? Where? With whom? Why? With what? and
When?"

He increased his pace in order to join the funeral procession more closely and stumbled in the process.

"So let us begin with *Quis?*"

The white ring-wall of Welgevonden's cemetery shone in
the distance; the wheels of the undertaker's black Cadillac
gouged holes in the grass, they churned up the black peat, they
rocked the glassed hearse with the colorful wreaths up and
down like a ship and forced the pallbearers out of line. The
faces of those in the procession were white against the black
of their clothes — a uniform white and black which would
only later, outside the context of the procession, become recognizable as individuals who, according to Dr. Johns, would
have to be considered one by one. It was a protective moment: nothing dared interrupt the procession — even if the
unknown Who? were to beat his breast and acknowledge his
deed. It was a moment of rest which everyone shared with the
deceased object in the hearse.

The service was taken by the Reverend Williams in the in-
tersectarian chapel sequestered in a corner of Welgevonden.
Against the wall were copper plaques which indicated the
names of those who, before interment, had undergone the
diversity of rituals intersectarially. Reverend Williams had,

in this instance, taken the service because the denomination
had been doubtful: the deceased had not been connected to
any faith, the choice had fallen on a genial Protestant sect, the
oration had been a model of free rhetoric, unconstrained by
dogma. It was a lyrical sermon by the intense pastor in his
neat little black suit: a genial summary of an unknown life
hovering, like all of us, between salvation and the clutch of
evil. The deceased had been loved (and everyone present,
guilty and innocent, knew how guilty or innocent the love
relationship) . . . A young girl in the flush of her life, *l'in-
connue* brought low when so much lay ahead of her . . .

Of Lila, the deceased daughter of the deceased whore with
the white face.

"Inspect them one by one," Dr. Johns said to Detective-
Sergeant Demosthenes H. de Goede, "but confine your impressions to the superficial." The hearse began its winding
route as the hill grew steeper, all along the contours, to prevent undue wear to the gearbox. "Don't get to know them too
well; stop short at the edge of consciousness." The hearse followed the contour line and, with its first turn, inadvertently
formed a somber question mark: the loop above, then the
stem, and right at the bottom the dot, where the giant, a little
behind it, was finding pleasure in the procession. "The deeper
you scratch," said Dr. Johns, "the deeper you go into the
mists."

The sun had disappeared behind the clouds, everything had
dimmed to the grayness that gave the right tone to a funeral
procession — a gray file which, with the second contour, had
a moment ago lost its question mark and made the line dis-
connected.

"For your purpose the superficial truth is the most important," said Dr. Johns, "because the deed was born at that level."

And now the black Cadillac began to circle around the circular white wall, around and around, to give the procession
cohesion, to satisfy the feeling for rhythm of the gray direc-
tor with his sable hat, until the multitude had been compelled
into *his* cycle and everything had come to a stop around the
Dingaan-kraal where the former inhabitants of Welgevonden
had been laid heterogeneously to rest: for there were the unknown, crumbled graves with slate headstones of God knew
who, *and* the angels of the Léfèbres, *and* the star of Juda isolated in its own *Bet Chayyim, and* Lila's open waiting grave.
Green raffia simulated a lawn between the clay, limestone and
black peat. (The soil there was extremely unsuitable for culti-
vation.) Bars with copper knobs lent an air of stylish swank,
the raked gravel ensured neatness, whitewashed bricks bor-
dered the footpaths, artificial flowers perpetuated their illusion in indestructible plastic. The doors of the hearse were
opened, they swung open and the imbuia coffin, handsome
with proteas, slid soundlessly out into the waiting hands of
the bearers who bent double to receive the weight of wood
and copper that encased slight Lila. For a moment they hesitated, determining sunrise and coffin direction, and then, at a
hint from the man in the top hat and frock coat, they found
sequence and direction and laid the coffin gratefully, swaying,
on the canvas strips over the gaping grave.

It grew darker, drizzle clouds clustered in the distance,
there was a cloud over Heuningberg, Reverend Williams lifted
up his eyes unto the cumulus and asked, "From whence com-
eth my help . . . ?"

An unknown bystander found his thoughts wandering; he did not feel in the least involved in the proceedings. He went through all the motions and all the requirements of the ritual, but he was actually more conscious of himself and his own feelings. I am moved, he thought, but is it *I* who am moved? The heat is damp and sticky. Someone is weeping. I look at the people and wonder what they are feeling. That one, for instance, with his eyes closed and an expression of dedication on his face. Is he thinking of the same things as I am, or is he listening to Reverend Williams?

"I knew Lila well," said Dr. Johns to Detective-Sergeant Demosthenes H. de Goede, and his voice sounded so loud that a number of people looked up.

There were few family around the grave except for an uncle from Welkom who had come over specially for the occasion, and an aunt with silver-blond hair dressed in black, in the finest silk stockings and with the prettiest ankles, and an uncle from the Karroo, with a rugged face, and a fat girl who wept and wept, ceaselessly, until her face looked like a little sow's.

"Lila was loved by all," said Dr. Johns more softly.

Lila was a bitch who came to bed like a virgin, every time (thought someone else). There she lies, defenseless and who can say that she was defenseless. Or . . . (he bit his knuckles) was I really the first? He looked around him and found everyone unworthy. Pure, undefiled Lila . . . his memories began all over again, differently, and he embalmed her in his heart.

Detective-Sergeant Demosthenes H. de Goede had a question clear and ready in his thoughts. He wished to put it to Dr. Johns and struggled in silence against his impediment of speech. As soon as he had a sentence clear, as soon as his thoughts were clear, everything would appear clear and distinct. The process of thought was simply the conversion of clear thinking into speech. He turned to Dr. Johns.

"Pssssst!" he said. "Ptttt . . . ttttt . . ."

Dr. Johns held his head nearer to listen, while a hymn was begun. He said something which was inaudible in the noise. His eyes followed the drizzle which was falling and appeared to be coming nearer.

Somebody should speak on behalf of the family, but the uncle from Welkom, the aunt and the farmer from the Karroo, felt like strangers. They had come from three remote corners, attracted by an obscure family sentiment, encouraged by that incomprehensible compulsion of conscience which caused relations to appear at funerals like specters, thereafter never to be seen or heard of again. They were simply there with questioning eyes, searching the faces around them, as if there they would find certainty about their own origin. And then, if perhaps they met someone who was of the family, they would nod their heads up and down; but the anxious, searching eyes would not change.

Then Reverend Williams began to speak on behalf of them all. It was an eloquent, persuasive flow of words, his facts based on fleeting observations and a prior chat here and there. In the little chapel Lila had been the subject for a text; here he had to depict her finally as someone who had existed, for the benefit of those who had known her better than himself. While he spoke, he looked at the faces around him, expressionless faces that gave no sign of his blunders. He depicted her as an orphan, an attractive, pretty, exemplary girl who had been loved by everyone, who had grown up among them, who had charmed everyone, who had died a violent death at the hands of a sadist who (God help him) would have to account before the Judgment Seat.

"But let us forget all these unpleasant things and remember her as we all knew her . . ."

The rain was coming nearer, softly, glancing over the heather to release him. He followed the blur with his eyes as he spoke. Heavens, he had never seen her, he did not know what she looked like, he knew only the two dates: the beginning and the end.

He ended his sermon with thanks to all those present. "Some have come far. As far as Welkom in the Orange Free State." (And the unknown uncle dropped his head.) He thought of her late mother with whom she would now be reunited and he left them inadvertently with the thought of the whore in heaven — the white-faced girl of eighteen years ago who had died in the extramarital birth of Lila.

The first drops now began to fall, imperceptibly at first, soft and soothing. The coffin sank with rocking movements. The mourners pressed forward and glanced over each other's shoulders. The little bowl of rose petals was handed around by the man in the top hat. Someone began to sob on hearing the words "unto dust shalt thou return . . ." Many hands seized the petals and sent them fluttering down into the darkness.

And nobody cried harder than Madam Ritchie and her two

daughters, Hope and Prudence. They were entitled to weep. They had the right to feel broken, because none had defamed Lila more than the three of them. The tears cascaded down the cheeks of the stout woman, who was buttressed on either side by her eighteen-year-old daughters (pretty, blond-haired girls with plaits and Viking eyes). At this last moment they gave Lila a tremendous farewell, while the rain increased. They were three lamenting women from a Greek drama: a classical symbol on the stage of the hill, against the gray sky.

Just before they dispersed they made room unwillingly for the Giant, the dot at the end of the procession when it was a question mark. He had just reached the place, he regarded the scene, forced his way through the people, grabbed the last rose petals in his big hand and let them fall one by one, watching each petal attentively until it vanished into the shadows. A last petal, damp from the rain, still stuck to his hand; he removed it carefully, shook it and let it fall meticulously into the depth.

When the rain began to fall harder, and everyone hurried back to the buildings of Welgevonden, with Jock and "slim" Mrs. Silberstein in the lead, Dr. Johns turned to Detective-Sergeant Demosthenes H. de Goede and said: "Remember the technical heptameter. If you are unable to abide by the sequence, then confine yourself at least to the requirements: the person, the fact, the place, the means, the motive, the manner and the time."

*

That night it rained so hard in the mountains that all the streams overflowed their banks and consequently cut Welgevonden off completely from the outside world. Throughout the night the masks bellowed as the waters rushed through their mouths. For days on end they dominated the landscape of Welgevonden — because they had found their voices.

QUIS? · Chapter Two · Through
the Eye of the Leopard ·· (Image of
light and shadow, of leaves moving, of waters,
of human figures, of flickerings in the dark; images
that come and go without rational connection. Partly
nature, partly thought process, partly feeling. Subhuman perceptions from deep in the unconscious: the differentiated I
peering over the partition and repeatedly sinking back into
formless primordialism. Levels of thought-energy that sink
through all the layers of consciousness to the charcoal, past
that, deeper and farther back where everything is amorphous
and then, recklessly, to take the form-creating step, to shoot
through all the layers to the top and to explode with all-embracing perception in the consciousness. A synthesis of opposites, a mystical experience, indescribable, a moment of hesitation between the divine and the demoniac, and then a grand-
iose, uncommunicable experience . . . released from the
talons of hell, the feeling of unity experienced in the heav-
enly unification.

The eye of the leopard through which the imbecile and
saints and poets and writers look; the mutation, the mental
defect, the divergent gene that has the same effects as mesca-
line, LSD and psyliciben, that unlocks the portals and makes
the perceptions big and intense, that brings inner freedom.
What difference that the unlocking is banal: the authenticity
and the quality of the feeling is beyond the stigma of the
means. In the face of this experience there is no difference in
the stature of the individual; and the idiot, the feebleminded,
can experience the eternal — he, too.)

To be one with the leaves all around, above, everywhere, moving; with the sunshine and the light in gradations of all colors that glittered on all imaginable forms; and which filled you continually with that ecstasy which you experienced many years ago as a young child and which still continued to live in poignant memories when you contemplated a mountain, a forest, a stream of water, an aspect of nature that had left its imprint on that first, wonderful, magical day many years ago.

Images and impressions of Welgevonden that came and went. Was there ever a dark-eyed mother whom you saw, felt and heard and of whom you were a part? Was it only later that you heard the name Salome, or had it been with you from the beginning? Was she part of that paradise, or did you go and fetch her where images welled up from the inexhaustible spring? And that big man who followed you continually with his tormenting eyes, where did he come from? And how do you reach him, the one who wakens love in you but whom you can never find?

Those were all questions and problems that only half troubled you as you floated on the steam of consciousness, as you looked into the green shadows cast by arum lilies, as you hid in tunnels of blue winds, as you slept coolly in caves of paper flowers, as you climbed the ladders of autumn-colored vines against white walls. In your idiot-brain there was something that isolated this paradise forever; you knew only the fear of intruders, of someone who removed you inopportunely, of those who disturbed the overpowering peace, rest and ecstasy with meaningless words and incomprehensible tasks. But, even though they took you away, you carried the paradise invisibly with you — and, close beside it, the intimation of chaos; you took them with you to the room with cloud-gray walls (when the key grated in the door); everywhere, you knew two worlds of experience and they could not exclude you. You were much bigger than they; you could break down the door, if you wished; you could, if you wished, destroy everything and everyone: just as you wished to destroy that apparition who came with anxiety, when that specter appeared at the window between the waving curtains, with her glowing eyes (her black eyes) that looked at you and you fought against her exhausting embrace until at last you submitted as you were emptied, and lay powerless while she grew warm and soft with satisfaction. She bit you with her sharp teeth, her breath smelled of blood, her body trembled against yours, she groaned from the depths in the darkness.

You recovered more slowly than she; as your strength returned you wished to destroy her, as soon as you rid yourself of your loneliness — but then it was too late; by then she had already gone, and you fumbled in vain in the dark and tore the pillow to tatters until rapture again predominated and you felt one with everything, and you sank down into unknown worlds where, suddenly, arum lilies and moonflowers swayed before your eyes, and little trumpet flowers with purple throats sounded small, thin notes against the pale blue air.

You washed yourself in the water that burbled on its way to the fountain. (It chatted over the stones; round, enticing sounds that came from everywhere.) You wedged your feet on either side of the masks, pressed your body against their mouths and strained against the stream. The talking water splashed off your body, arched over your shoulders and soared against the sun. Then you were purified of taint.

But tonight, in your room, you longed again for black chaos and peeped at the window with the waving curtains. You were filled with trepidation, but waited nevertheless for the phosphorescent glow. You were used to it, for as long as you could remember. She would always be there; you had always the same intentions and you were always just too late. It had been thus all your life, and so it would always be in that system of shocking contrasts.

Today the world was wet. Your tracks lay deep in the earth. You wandered over the virginal grass and despoiled the earth. The whole world was fresh and full of sunshine. You felt free and your head swam when you saw the open landscape.

Then you saw the two of them. They darkened the landscape. You stooped and cupped black, muddy soil in your hands; you pressed it into a round, yielding ball of clay. (It awoke memories in you; it lived tremblingly in your hands.) Then you hurled it with all your strength at the intruders.

The clay disintegrated in the air and disappeared on the grass. But no matter: the feeling of frustration was temporary; there were moonflowers waiting; there was a wall to climb. There was the dark cave of red, brown and purple flowers. There was no end to that ecstasy. You rose above everybody. You were part of the paradise. You would crush them like ants. You raised your hands in the air; already you had wings.

You flew; you flew so high that you could no longer even hear them. Your enormous hands could exterminate them; but there were so many things you had to do; there was so much to attract you, there was so much music in the water that already you had forgotten about them.

QUIS? · Chapter Three · To Look
Down into a Drained Pool . . . ·· The
clod disintegrated in the air and fell in a spray
of sand and lumps of mud on the grass. Dr. Johns
pointed his finger in admonition in the direction of the
thrower and smiled at Detective-Sergeant Demosthenes H. de
Goede.

"Adam Kadmon Silberstein!" he called, and the Giant stood
still. They saw at first only his cumbersome back, the shirt
that clung in wrinkles to the sweaty, wet body, the figure
camouflaged by the shrubs. They could see from his posture
that he was listening: from the slight tenseness, from the way
in which the shoulders were drawn askew and became a sensitive organ that moved lightly to and fro.

"Adam Kadmon Silberstein!" Dr. Johns repeated, and the
Giant turned around and laughed at them.

It came as a shocking contrast: from behind he was a grotesque colossus of eight feet four inches, a monstrous deviation
from the normal, something one associated with the circus,
or the sports field, or a spectacle from a film dreamed up in
Los Angeles — but now, from the front, one saw a boy of
eighteen who, guilty and abashed, laughed with long, sharp
teeth — a serrated set of adolescent teeth.

"*Ossians, dentes candide* . . ." said Dr. Johns. He beckoned to the giant, who came forward a few paces reluctantly
and then stopped again.

He had red hair, blue eyes and a pale complexion. Whereas,
in a dwarf, one was struck by the old face in the body of a
child, here the effect was the opposite: the young face in the
monstrous body. His movements were clumsy, like those

of someone not able to coordinate the use of his limbs properly, but his strength was disturbing. In his right hand he held a large piece of a log which he jerked nervously up and down with his left hand until it broke in two with a cracking sound. The next moment he jerked at the other, shorter piece until it, too, crumbled after a short while in his mighty left hand. His eyes were never still; he looked around him often, and as often his attention was distracted by something else — the setter running across the grass ("Fido! Fido!"), or something that crackled in the bushes. When the piece of log had been crumbled to powder and nothing of it was left, he sought with restless hands for something to do. When Dr. Johns walked nearer and took him by the arm, he reacted like a naughty child and slapped the outstretched arm rudely away — the awkward gesture of a child, but with uncontrolled force behind it. Dr. Johns gave him a handful of sugar candy and he stuffed all into his mouth. As he ate, his cheeks distended, he looked at the Detective-Sergeant with sly eyes and an expression of mischievous naughtiness.

"Pssssttt . . . fffffft . . ." came Demosthenes H. de Goede's stuttering attempt to make contact, and the giant suddenly doubled up in the madness of a hysterical fit of laughter, his mouth wide open so that the candy spattered out, and his body swayed to and fro, his eyes bulging. The next moment he ran away; but after a short distance came to a stop again. He looked back and there was no aftermath of his fit of laughter. He simply looked at them with his empty eyes and then he seemed to be looking for something, for someone, to join him in his lonely world.

The dog attracted his attention and the two of them disappeared quickly toward the fountain and the noisy masks against the mountainside.

"A lamentable case," said Dr. Johns as they wandered on toward the Welgevonden homestead. "His mother was a lovely woman, Salome, Jock Silberstein's daughter. He came to the light like a tiger and lacerated her. She pampered him for seven days before she died. An infant of fifteen pounds is not yet a monster."

He looked at the house among the trees, at the gables that rose like a village above the branches.

"You should have seen the farm then. It was a wonderful place. The Silbersteins lived like princes."

They approached the swimming pool.

"She died before she had had the *mikvah*," said Dr. Johns.

The swimming pool was empty.

"But the *chevra kaddisha* washed, prepared and clothed her properly in a pure white *kittel*. Salome with the dark eyes. She was a legendary beauty. Do those words mean anything to you?"

The cement was dry and crumbling. Cracks made black lines between the whitewashed sides. The swimming pool had been built to Olympic specifications but, empty as it now was, it looked like a meaningless excavation. Weeds and nettles grew on the bottom; there was the excrement of humans and animals in one corner; silt was building up against the farthest side. After the rain everything was moist and fermenting in the subsequent heat. The sour smell of active decomposition assailed them.

"How can I describe her to you?" said Dr. Johns as they

sat down on the edge of the pool, their ankles thudding against the brittle plaster. "Intelligent, full of love and compassion for her husband. The perfect wife who, apparently, gave up everything for the mystical togetherness, yet nevertheless held something back: the mystery in which the godlike and the earthly were woven together. We all desired her with longing and pride because we knew that the longing and desire of nobody else would be satisfied. Perhaps she was a figment of our imagination, and their togetherness the romantic dream of all of us. But was it a dream?"

Dr. Johns' age was unknown. He looked like a small baboon on the edge of the empty swimming pool: a shrunken piece of facile wisdom that created and destroyed illusions; full of energy resulting from correct diet and exercise, a wiry example of pertinacity, an eloquent example of an old body that with sustained effort might still, after perhaps its eightieth year, one fierce, sweating night, make a virgin fall pregnant, to prove the pathos of human diligence.

"She was married to a Christian, Henry van Eeden," said Dr. Johns. "The Van Eedens had the prestige, the Silbersteins the money. It was an ideal conjunction and a triumph for the calculating machine. But then she gave birth to a mentally deficient giant."

The man beside him began to stutter.

(Detective-Sergeant Demosthenes H. de Goede was the product of one of the best police colleges in the country. He had done particularly well in all his examinations. In spite of his speech impediment he passed *cum laude* and, also physically, came up to standard by, for instance, running the mile in just over four minutes. He was an excellent pistol shot. He knew Gardener's Law of Evidence by rote.)

"And Henry van Eeden is one of the best read and most intelligent people I know," said Dr. Johns. "Do you know the basic facts about heredity?"

A cloud obscured the sun and passed on, but the pool remained empty. One could not imagine that it had ever been full of water; one could not believe in a time when people had swum and gamboled in it with those idiot sounds which denoted pleasure.

"In the moronic child, heredity plays an important part," said Dr. Johns, "but in the case of imbeciles and idiots the intelligence quotient of the parents is unimportant. In Adam Kadmon the aberrant gene probably developed by means of a new mutation in the germ cell of one of the parents. It happens once in fifty thousand cases, and nobody is to blame. It's a comfort to Jock Silberstein: there is no stain on the forebears; the true seed of tragedy is present here, because there can be no blame."

In a corner of the swimming pool the nettles moved without visible agent. It could have been a snake, a rat or some big insect. The leaves seemed to have a life of their own. Demosthenes H. de Goede threw a stone in that direction. He had aimed well, because the stone fell in the middle of the plant. Immediately the movement stopped, but the crown of the plant had been knocked off.

"Is it possible that the idiot-giant could have committed the murder?" asked Dr. Johns.

Detective-Sergeant Demosthenes H. de Goede struggled to answer.

"Usually there are also visible deviations in the physical composition of the idiot child," said Dr. Johns. "But Adam Kadmon is superficially normal, like a moron; only his I.Q. is that of an idiot. The fact that he is a giant has nothing to do with his backwardness."

Dr. Johns' face was finely wrinkled. His little eyes flickered between the folds, his bald pate gleamed in the sun. "Is Adam Kadmon a Klinefelter case? Was Lila raped before she was murdered? The Klinefelter's genitals have not developed normally. If we had the answers to those two questions we would have progressed far."

Detective-Sergeant Demosthenes H. de Goede took out his notebook and made notes in it. His handwriting was particularly neat, as if in compensation for his speech defect. The form of the entries in his notebook was a calligraphic work of art. He sighed and returned the book to his jacket pocket.

"Adam Kadmon is a hypophyseal giant," said Dr. Johns. "No retrogressive gene is present here. Everything is a product of the mucous gland of the brain and is not hereditary. They usually grow weaker with increasing age. He will probably not grow older than twenty years."

They heard something and looked down. Suddenly the pool began to fill before their eyes. In the past there had been a pump that alternately emptied and refilled the pool; pressure had apparently cleared a blockage and after many years the water bubbled in again.

Dr. Johns had stopped talking and he and Detective-Sergeant Demosthenes H. de Goede stared fascinated at the rising water, their eyes held by the deluge scene of thousands of little creatures that appeared from among the weeds and drifted, wriggling, about. A single weed drifted to the surface. It was the broken-off crown of the stinging nettle spiraling up toward the sunlight. Presently they had to lift their feet, so fast did the water rise. When the pool was full, the water stopped rising: the pumping system was in working order again; after so many hours the pool would be emptied and then, most likely, refilled.

From a clump of trees a group of children came running over the lawn, as if they had been in telepathic communication with the pool. They all wore bathing suits and tumbled one by one into the water. There was shrieking, horseplay and noise. The water splashed over the sides and insects and excrement littered the adjoining grass. The entire world shuddered and lived with the clamor and hooting of the children.

Dr. Johns and Detective-Sergeant Demosthenes H. de Goede stood for a moment looking at them until they were overcome by that deep boredom which assails everyone who watches children in a swimming pool; then, depressed, they walked away and down to the Welgevonden homestead.

"Adam Kadmon will have to be investigated," said Dr. Johns. "And Lila will have to be disinterred."

QUIS? · Chapter Four · The Api-
koros ·· It was he who appeared there
before them: the *Mayofis* Jew who sought to
accommodate himself in the Diaspora by means of a
social and spiritual flirtation, who had built his pathetic
castle to assure himself of a home there, who shone with geni-
ality and, through his unlimited love, went farther astray.

"Jock Silberstein, our host," said Dr. Johns and stretched
out his arms as if to embrace them both, draw them nearer
and reconcile them in one single, important endeavor. "Detective-Sergeant Demosthenes H. de Goede, charged with the
investigation."

Detective-Sergeant Demosthenes H. de Goede stuttered his
expressions of goodwill with clear-sounding, meaningless
vowels and consonants and received a firm handshake that he
avenged with all the power at his disposal.

(Demosthenes H. de Goede had been not only a good ath-
lete in the conventional sense at the police college, but was
known for being able to lift a billiard stick from the floor with
his index and middle fingers.)

They were directly in front of the door of the Silbersteins'
house: the gables arched on either side, the Bacchus-figures
poured their overabundance of fruit and wine motionlessly in
hard whitewash.

"Have you seen Adam Kadmon?" asked Jock Silberstein
and he peered over their shoulders toward the lawn that vanished expansively in the distance.

"We have just seen him," said Dr. Johns. "He has probably
gone to swim in the stream by the masks and has taken his
daily ablution."

"Is the stream not too strong?" asked Jock Silberstein anxiously.

The rumble of the water could be heard clearly.

"He is strong," said Dr. Johns.

And to each of them came the vision of the giant figure against the stream.

"This morning he took my hand," said Jock Silberstein, "and he asked after Lila. He does not realize that she is dead."

"He loved Lila very much," said Dr. Johns and looked meaningly at Demosthenes H. de Goede.

"He came to me," said Jock Silberstein, "without my having done anything. He did not pull away. He came to me of his own volition and took my hand. And then he asked after Lila." He, too, looked at Demosthenes H. de Goede and explained: "He loved her and does not realize that she is dead. This morning he came to me and took my hand and asked: 'Where is Lila?'"

It was as if the waters, after the incessant rain of the previous day, were murmuring everywhere all over Welgevonden.

"He is strong," said Jock Silberstein. "The stream will not easily carry him away. He takes hold on either side of the masks and then he lets the water wash over him."

"Tremendous muscles," said Dr. Johns.

"The strength of a lion," said Jock Silberstein. "And a loving, tender heart. He would not harm a person or an animal." He prepared to leave but decided otherwise. "The strong are as meek as lambs. They understand their own strength." His face brightened. "They don't have to prove themselves."

They all remained quiet for a moment.

"Lila loved him," said Jock Silberstein. "They were part of Welgevonden. The whole family. Her great-grandmother and father, her mother and her . . ." He smiled suddenly. "She could have been my child, d'you know, Dr. Johns?"

"And mine," said Dr. Johns.

They seemed to have forgotten about Demosthenes H. de Goede. The Welgevonden of eighteen years ago was being lived again, but at that time Demosthenes H. de Goede was still at school.

"Her mother was a remarkable girl," said Dr. Johns. "It's strange that she died at exactly the same age as her daughter. Both were eighteen years old. If you could imagine a hereafter, then they would meet each other as equals. Two girls of eighteen."

"A mother and daughter of the same age with the same appearance and the same past," said Jock Silberstein. "Just imagine!"

"A mutual echo," said Dr. Johns.

"A sort of repetition," said Jock Silberstein.

They looked past each other in opposite directions and fell into a peaceful silence. Dr. Johns' eyes were lost among the neglected trees that checkmated one another before the house, where, like giants, they were destroying one another; Jock Silberstein peered intently across the lawn toward the distant masks.

"Well," he said suddenly, "I think I'll wander off toward the fountain. Perhaps I'll find Adam Kadmon there." He turned to Detective-Sergeant Demosthenes H. de Goede. "Enjoy your stay."

Demosthenes H. de Goede raised his hat gallantly and bowed to his host. He and Dr. Johns walked silently up to the enormous front door of the enormous house.

"Actually, an unbelieving Jew," said Dr. Johns. "But every so often he does something to establish a connection. And sometimes it's the most unexpected and odd things: the making of a *shema*, for instance," and he pointed to a metal container built into the right of the front door. He lifted the ornamental knocker and rapped three times with a musical rhythm. "A lewd romantic with a longing to both sides. Is that not perhaps the true nature of the puritan?"

Footsteps sounded in the passage. Dr. Johns rapped on the metal container. "The first two paragraphs of the *shema* written, rolled up and built in by himself. Perhaps soon after he had slept one night with Lila. It wasn't here a month ago."

The door opened and a Malay maid peeped out. She smiled when she saw Dr. Johns. She had two pure white false front teeth, disproportionately big in comparison with the others, with a small ruby added on the starboard side.

"Because a relationship between a married man and an unmarried woman was not considered as adultery," said Dr. Johns, and smiled back.

They waited in the front hall while the maid went in search of their hostess and sat on two of a row of chairs that filled the whole hall. Everywhere there were pieces of furniture and old chests, polished and shiny with rubbing, pushed together and arranged in unlivable order, as in the inner rooms of the Koopmans de Wet Museum. They looked through the door and saw the garden through which they had recently passed: the flowers overcrowded by weeds, the trees full of dead branches as, unpruned, they throttled one another — all in complete contrast to the neat lawn in the distance. And then their attention returned to the room in which they sat waiting, to the stairs at the bottom end of the passage, the dark rails, the huge furniture, the antiques that were now entirely part of the past. Here, in spite of everything, there was no dilapidation. The dissolution was overpolished, the disintegration arrested by varnish and lacquer.

"I wish you could have seen the place eighteen years ago," said Dr. Johns. "But that was before the Silbersteins gave the place to the Foundation."

Detective-Sergeant Demosthenes H. de Goede at once stuttered a question.

"After the birth of the Giant," said Dr. Johns, "Jock Silberstein gave the greater part of the house and all the lands to the Foundation, and kept back the front part of the house for himself and his wife. I'll show you the rest of the house later; they occupy the front rooms."

He pointed to the furniture.

"That's why the place is so chockablock. And three-quarters of the other antiques are decaying in storerooms." He looked at his watch. "I wonder what's keeping her." He sighed and stretched himself out in the chair. "The Silbersteins lived in the whole place themselves in the old days. Forty, fifty guests at a time was nothing unusual. The place crawled with people and roared with voices. The entire farm was a model of activity — a factory with and without walls."

He looked up when he heard the servant girl coming. "And

then he gave it to the Foundation and everything changed."

They stood up and followed the servant down another passage to a big room on the right.

On the way Dr. Johns asked Detective-Sergeant Demosthenes H. de Goede for his opinion on why Jock Silberstein had given everything to the Foundation. He answered his own question when he found himself dissatisfied with the reasons as he interpreted them from the stuttering sounds.

"They could have accepted the death of Salome and the birth of the Giant without doing that. They could have accepted the double disaster as part of life: the up and down . . . What happens when, suddenly, after a time, a whole way of life ceases to exist? You accept it that way. It just ceases." The servant opened the double doors of the room. "Or did Jock Silberstein perhaps, like a realist, destroy everything to ensure permanence?"

And now, as the servant girl disappeared soundlessly, they confronted a huge hall that had once upon a time been a magnificent place of assembly, but had now become a warehouse for all those things that one collects over the years and does not have the heart to get rid of.

There were a few valuable pieces that survived the rubbish and would come into their own in different circumstances, but they now became indistinguishable among the involuntary baroque. Then there were other pieces that derived their value from memories and from all the unpredictable love of human beings, but that now showed their intrinsic worthlessness under the glare of objectivity. There was actually something pathetic about that untidy room. And precisely in that lay the triumph of ordinary small things: that everything be-

came ordinary and that the hideous, gilded nude girl with a
clock in her navel could stand in equality with a seventeenth-
century escritoire.

At the far end, against the wall, they observed "slim" Mrs.
Silberstein before an oval wall mirror in which she was studying herself. They saw her inspect herself from all angles as
they approached: from below, above, the sides and over her
shoulder. As they drew nearer, unseen, and stood by her, she
used a hand mirror as well. They even saw their own images
in the looking glass: slim and elegant in the mirror-illusion.
But — in her abandonment, in the blindness of her liturgy —
she was unaware of them.

And then she began her exercises at leisure: a dance for the
sake of rhythm and her figure. The *apache* Mrs. Silberstein
with the guttersnipe expression on her face and blue circles
painted around her eyes. The dance of the menopause in a
heat of its own that scorched her cheeks.

"Mrs. Silberstein," said Dr. Johns, and she dropped the
hand mirror, which splintered on the floor.

She changed before their eyes; she turned around and became stout and square in front, and slim and elegant behind.

"Demosthenes H. de Goede, the Detective-Sergeant charged
with the investigation — Mrs. Silberstein," said Dr. Johns
and bowed away his embarrassment impartially between
them.

Mrs. Silberstein recovered swiftly and regained her calm.

"Seven years' bad luck," she said and pointed to the shattered pieces of the hand mirror that Demosthenes de Goede
was gallantly scratching together. "Put them there," she said
vaguely and looked at him with interest.

"Detective-Sergeant Demosthenes H. de Goede," Dr. Johns repeated, "here in connection with the death of Lila."

"What a tragic happening!" said "slim" Mrs. Silberstein and sank down gracefully in one of the Louis XV chairs. "So pretty and young, and yet . . ." She smiled charmingly at Dr. Johns. "Could one expect anything else after the sort of life she led?"

Demosthenes H. de Goede remained standing uncertainly with the glass splinters in his hand. *"There!"* she said and admired his broad shoulders as he arranged the splinters in a neat little heap on one of the tables. "And what is your impression, Mr. de Goede?"

"The Detective-Sergeant is simply still getting acquainted with all the people," said Dr. Johns, who also had found himself a seat. "Welgevonden is surrounded by water and the criminal is cornered. Your use of the word 'tragic' is entirely correct." He nodded to Detective-Sergeant Demosthenes H. de Goede who was staring irresolutely at the collection of chairs. "The misdemeanor has been committed, the ordained deed has been done. The tragic unity is present. Somewhere the mark of the immutable personality of the miscreant has been made. Detective-Sergeant de Goede represents order, the ethical view of life of us all." He smiled at Demosthenes H. de Goede who, at the moment, was busy flicking the remaining, finer chips from his hands with a silk handkerchief. "It's a transgression against God and the community, we have lost our innocence, Paradise is threatened and we demand retaliation through Detective-Sergeant de Goede, so that we may regain Paradise."

"Slim" Mrs. Silberstein pressed one of the knobs on the wall and waited until the servant girl appeared with a trolley of drinks. Both she and Dr. Johns drank wine. Detective-Sergeant Demosthenes H. de Goede preferred brandy and water with, yes, a little ice.

"They all slept with the little bitch," said "slim" Mrs. Silberstein. "Is her body softer because she is young? Does she appear different? Does she feel different just because she is young?" She looked at Dr. Johns who acknowledged his implied complicity proudly, with a rueful inclination of the head. "She had little intelligence," said "slim" Mrs. Silberstein impatiently, "and almost no personality. A proper little milksop." Her eyes shone fervently and it was easy to imagine the unattractiveness of age gone, and to believe the colorful cosmetics in the dim light. The consort of Ashmodai was still ardent enough to inspire amulets and incantations. Her mood distorted her face, like the masks, and Detective-Sergeant Demosthenes H. de Goede showed his willingness purposelessly to satisfy her slightest whim.

"Everything is *so* confused," said "slim" Mrs. Silberstein, suddenly calm. "What can we do with all this furniture?"

She looked around helplessly.

"That Nederburg baroque wall cupboard, for instance — it's blocking the view through the window . . ."

Detective-Sergeant Demosthenes H. de Goede, with a mighty movement of his shoulders, arms and hands, moved the heavy cupboard to the left, and the valuable porcelain inside broke with a tinkle.

"And the curvilinear Meerlust yellowwood cupboard . . ."

said "slim" Mrs. Silberstein as she sank back deeper in the chair
and her whole body followed the next muscular movement
that shifted the empty cupboard three feet to the right and
let in a small patch of sunlight and landscape; because now
they could see the lawn in the distance and hear more clearly
the noise of the waters rushing through the invisible masks.

"Speaking of the personality of the murderer," said Dr.
Johns; "I read somewhere that the I.Q. of murderers is exceptionally low. It has been determined in certain institutions
that the average is only seventy-one — about the same as a
smart moron." He looked meaningly at Detective-Sergeant
Demosthenes H. de Goede who, somewhat out of breath,
stood beside the cupboard. "But that is, of course, not so in
all cases. It hangs together with the fact that the murderer
generally has not enough intelligence to foresee the conse-
quences of his or her deed."

"In that case our poor Adam Kadmon is probably first on
the list," said "slim" Mrs. Silberstein, but she said it in such a
way as to suggest that she attached little value to it. Her attention was rather on Detective-Sergeant Demosthenes H. de
Goede, who had in the meantime quieted down. "You no
doubt took a considerable part in athletics and displays of
strength, Mr. de Goede?"

Detective-Sergeant Demosthenes H. de Goede had, among
other things, been a wrestling champion as well, and in his
spare time at college taken a course of Charles Atlas, according to which muscle-building was achieved by means of
spiritual concentration and contramuscular tension. Via
Dr. Johns he received enthusiastic permission from "slim" Mrs.

Silberstein to explain by way of demonstration, and for a start
he removed his jacket and then his shirt carefully. The clothing was put neatly on the window seat and the tie hung over a
chair. He was tanned a handsome brown and his muscles
moved supplely together at the slightest movement of his arms
and body. He put his right fist in the palm of his left hand,
strained all his powers, pushed, and the next moment the muscles moved beneath his skin as if they were charged with elec-
tricity. His entire torso quivered in merciless tension, which
increased together with the breathless admiration of "slim"
Mrs. Silberstein. Waves of muscle careered across his arms,
collided with one another, swelled to bursting and vanished
immediately as he relaxed.

"With a woman the pattern of murder is naturally different," said Dr. Johns. "She sets about things more systematically. Her methods are indirect. The chances of her
being caught are fewer. Everything points to greater intelligence and, therefore, greater danger."

Detective-Sergeant Demosthenes H. de Goede was now
pushing with shorter intervals and there was a noticeable
rhythm in the way in which the tormented muscles collided
with one another.

"It's interesting," Dr. Johns continued, "that it is said of
Euripides' *Hippolytus* that the tragic hero is not an individual,
but man. The cosmic power is impersonal, the interplay of
good and evil is outside the control of the individual, the whole
community is the victim, the question of blame is secondary."

"Slim" Mrs. Silberstein, gripped by the muscle-play, began
to hum "The Blue Danube," and Demosthenes H. de Goede,

ready as usual, adapted himself to the rhythm of her accompaniment, so that his muscles swelled, collided and relaxed to triple time and in so doing surpassed the theory of the famed Atlas by crowning his dogma of concentration with musicology.

"As Philip Vellacott puts it in the foreword to his translation," said Dr. Johns, "at the stage when evil achieved the upper hand, it was already beyond the control of the human being. Something subhuman, superhuman, something impersonal, was involved . . ."

"Slim" Mrs. Silberstein was now sharing Detective-Sergeant Demosthenes H. de Goede's athletic ecstasy in a way that he naturally did not understand. (Our police colleges endorse with monasticism the celibate dedication to State and God respectively.)

"Something like the Fatum, the Moira, Fate," said Dr. Johns.

Detective-Sergeant Demosthenes H. de Goede now (at the insistence of "slim" Mrs. Silberstein) removed his vest, too, folded it up, put it away and exposed the whole of his torso on which the vertical and horizontal muscles of his stomach revealed another landscape and a jollier rhythm.

"The Giant," said Dr. Johns, "fits in so perfectly as an unfeeling implement of the supralogical that one should be inclined to detect a clue here, too."

Detective-Sergeant Demosthenes H. de Goede was now busy manipulating his central abdominal band. It was an impressive exhibition and within the power of only the greatest masters of the cult. First of all he took a deep breath, and then a deeper one, forced out his lungs in the top part of his chest, retracted his stomach to nothing and then to a cavity, and strained as hard as he could. A single, vertical muscle appeared: a phallic symbol which made "slim" Mrs. Silberstein share orgiastically in his triumph.

"Our only expedient," said Dr. Johns, "is to conceal ourselves, and, like Henry Silberstein-van Eeden — Mrs. Silberstein's son-in-law," he explained to Detective-Sergeant Demosthenes H. de Goede, who had suddenly lifted himself on his hands, his feet in the air, "our only expedient is to cultivate, like Henry Silberstein-van Eeden, astuteness. It is fatal to try and be heroic. We must accept Christian humility, turn the other cheek, protect ourselves with benevolence and make ourselves invisible by means of meekness."

Detective-Sergeant Demosthenes H. de Goede was surpassing himself. Not only was he standing on his hands, but he was balancing himself on the ten slim pillars of his fingers.

"Slim" Mrs. Silberstein had suspended all refinement, dropped all pretense of polish and crouched on her knees, like a little girl, before Detective-Sergeant Demosthenes H. de Goede who, achieving the impossible on an elegant index finger, withdrew nine of the little pillars.

"Only a heroic lunatic," said Dr. Johns desperately, "would destroy himself against the rock and refuse to capitulate. We must adapt ourselves to the spirit of the times."

"Slim" Mrs. Silberstein had just tickled Detective-Sergeant Demosthenes H. de Goede under his arms. She lay beside him on the floor, her eyes close to his face, which grew redder and redder with exertion as he tried to keep vertical and at the same time to resist the teasing of his risorial muscles. Suddenly he collapsed; their laughter rang through the room and they tumbled together in a heap in front of Dr. Johns who, silently and with interest now, watched the rudimentary seduction. But then, all of a sudden, "slim" Mrs. Silberstein straightened up, pushed her dress indolently back over garter, thigh and silk stocking, and ran her fingers through her hair.

"The poor Giant," said "slim" Mrs. Silberstein. "The poor scapegoat. One for the Lord and one for Azazel."

"I merely mentioned his name," said Dr. Johns in self-defense, "to exemplify an impersonal implement in the hand of an impersonal fate."

She stood up sluggishly and went to the looking glass, which lied flatteringly. She brought her face nearer to it as if searching for the answer to the riddle. Then she lightly touched herself under her eyes, on her temples and on her neck. Her face again became distorted, like the dripping masks that were noisy in the distance, but even that was reflected untruthfully as youthful melancholy; and in the background, like a bronze god in the looking glass, which clothed him in kingly garments, Demosthenes H. de Goede was carefully putting on, first, his vest, and then his shirt, tie and jacket.

"It could be any one of us," said Dr. Johns. "I admit that. Not one of us is invisible enough to escape the attention of evil."

He and Detective-Sergeant Demosthenes H. de Goede left the room in silence, after being dismissed by "slim" Mrs. Silberstein with a slight movement of her hand. Her back was turned squarely on them; her eyes, beautified by the looking glass, were fixed motionlessly on herself.

QUIS? · Chapter Five · The Residents: Madam, Hope and Prudence Ritchie ·· "Beyond this door," Dr. Johns said to Detective-Sergeant Demosthenes H. de Goede as they reached the end of a narrow passage, "the Foundation takes over. I trust that you'll immediately notice the difference."

They were now beside the house but were still surrounded by buildings connected to the original house by walls and passages. There were signs of the old bachelor quarters but it was difficult, without help, to single out the originals. The Department of Public Works had, in characteristic fashion, succeeded in obliterating all forms of style by means of extensions and additions. Here and there the Monuments Commission had put up its bronze plaques to identify, for a grateful posterity, the authentic: a handsomely shaped arch beam here, a ringwall there. The green bronze plaques (they were innumerable in that maze) indicated Old Cape architectonic oases in the official wilderness; it was an adventure for the cognoscente to have his supposition confirmed by the dogma of a plaque on a stone arch, an abutment or a cellar dome.

It was, for instance, by no means impossible that Dr. Johns had mistaken a plaque of the Monuments Commission for the *shema* beside the front door. It was, however, unlikely, since Detective-Sergeant Demosthenes H. de Goede had as one of his optional courses, "General Improvement," under *capita selecta*, made a study of "Religions of the World," and would immediately have pointed out the mistake to Dr. Johns.

"Have you noticed," asked Dr. Johns, "that Jock Silberstein

defended the Giant and that "slim" Mrs. Silberstein stood kindheartedly aloof? All attention is directed at Adam Kadmon, the stupid colossus. We are all moving in the shadow of the Giant."

They walked on in a vain attempt to see the house in perspective. Walls, rooms and outbuildings of all kinds turned them back time and time again to an inner circle of buildings.

"Do you know the legend of the Giants in mythology?" Dr. Johns asked suddenly.

Detective-Sergeant Demosthenes H. de Goede stuttered his knowledge.

"Exactly," said Dr. Johns. "The Giant Typhon resulted from the intercourse of Earth and Tartarus."

Unexpectedly they found a gate; they were once again on the rolling lawns that surrounded the house, and from where they stood they could understand better the nature of the alterations and additions. Here the Foundation had taken over completely and built on to such an extent that the architectural style of Public Works, freed from the Old Cape Dutch burden, had at last triumphed. There were brown doors and windows everywhere, covered with six or seven layers of paint to keep secret the material; dull, heavy and solid, one was reminded of station buildings or those brick-colored constructions on experimental farms. The trees before the windows were rare and indigenous and grew about half an inch a year to throw, after more than three hundred years, a proud shadow. The flowers in the beds were utterly regimented — but in a different manner to that of the old days at Welgevonden. There was no longer a mathematical cheerfulness; the sickly grew sicklier beside the strong that grew stronger, both under the vigilant eyes of botanists who specialized in both directions and found decay as fascinating as growth.

"I was actually thinking of the origin of the Giants who fought the gods," said Dr. Johns as, in their wandering, they looked at the rows of rooms and at the faces through the windows, hanging disembodied over desks.

"I was thinking of Gaea who encouraged her son, Cronus, to kill her husband, Uranus, while he was enjoying her."

They had now reached another lawn where Detective-Sergeant Demosthenes H. de Goede was confronted with Public Works in the guise of regeneration, under the influence of young architects who had traveled considerably abroad.

"Cronus emasculated his father with his left hand and threw his manhood into the sea," said Dr. Johns. "The style of the sixties," he explained in regard to the buildings that grimaced at them with hundreds of windows.

The new buildings looked like an American suburban paradise. The walls were of various colors, the steel frames chosen from the rich uniformity of a well-known catalog; each room faced the other squarely and the occupants, separated by large glass windows and patches of grass, lived outwardly and for one another.

"Cronus emasculated his father with a sickle," said Dr. Johns, "but his blood impregnated his mother and she gave birth to the Giants. To the Giants and to the Erinyes that will persecute until the end of time."

The residents looked at one another through the windows,

through the panes that like the lenses of cameras and binoculars were aimed from one side to the other.

"And then the struggle between the Olympian gods and the Giants originated," said Dr. Johns. "But like the Titans, the Giants, too, were doomed to destruction."

Behind a window sat a woman with many colored curlers in her hair. Her hair was pulled tightly against her skull and fastened with orange, yellow, blue, green and purple clips. She was in earnest conversation with a similar sort of woman. Suddenly they looked up, saw Dr. Johns and smiled with false teeth that gleamed through the glass.

Dr. Johns waved to them and was greeted with an increasing number of porcelain chips.

"But the most interesting of all is," said Dr. Johns, "that the Giants were actually primitive earthly spirits, and that they could only be destroyed by a magical plant. The plant that Hercules found in Erebus. Hercules who saves us from erotic nightmares: from the Giant Porphyrion who wished to rape Hera, from the Giant Pallas who wished to dishonor his own daughter, Pallas Athena."

Each apartment had a different color-mark of distinction and they stopped now before variations of blue. They went nearer and the resident approached them from behind a glass door.

"From revenge," said Dr. Johns, "Gaea slept with Tartarus and gave birth to the greatest Giant ever born, your monster Typhon. But he, too, was doomed to destruction."

The door opened and Dr. Johns said: "Allow me to introduce you, Madam Ritchie, to Detective-Sergeant Demosthenes H. de Goede."

A large woman filled the doorframe, raised her fat arms in a gesture of greeting, and stood aside for them to enter. Her head was a network of curlers and her face red and puffy, like that of a woman who had just come from under a hairdresser's dryer. She touched her hair and then regarded Demosthenes H. de Goede with friendly little eyes that, superficially, shone with pleasant acknowledgment but which, if one were attentive to the hidden glint behind the glance, held him for a moment in cold-blooded calculation and classified him according to her own Almanac.

"A pleasure, Mr. de Goede," she said and by means of the single word "Mister," allowed him — unknowing — into the inner circle. Had it been otherwise, she would have held him at a distance by repetition of the title "Detective-Sergeant."

(Detective-Sergeant Demosthenes H. de Goede's father was a farmer. During his final term at the police college, the ladies of the Sunrise Nurses' Hostel voted the Sergeant the most attractive cadet of the year, on the occasion of their Invitation Ball.)

He bent over her hand and thus gave her the opportunity of sending the mother-sign to her two daughters, Hope and Prudence, who were waiting in the background, in the no-man's-land of the passage.

Two appealing girls: the one athletic and strong of tooth; the other lissome and full breasted. Their fair hair, at this stage with the gleam of youthful growth, was combed to gleaming wave crests. Their lips were white, their skins bronzed by sunlight in their glass rooms.

Detective-Sergeant Demosthenes H. de Goede bowed to them with a smiling grimace that held a world of meaning for his fellows in age. They grinned back and contact on the time level had been made.

"I have just explained to Detective-Sergeant Demosthenes H. de Goede something about the true nature of the mythological Giants," said Dr. Johns. "The nightmare from the Unconscious, the terrifying primordial images that can be exorcised only by means of the magical plant and the intervention of the hero."

Madam Ritchie indicated that they should all be seated and nodded encouragingly at Dr. Johns, noticing with approval that her two daughters had taken their places side by side and were coquettishly ignoring the Detective-Sergeant.

"The erotic nature of the Giants is, of course, not unknown," said Dr. Johns, flattered by the attention suddenly accorded him. "For instance, it is not for nothing that the name of the leader of the Giants, Ephialtes, means *incubus* in Latin." He was a little disturbed that there was no reaction. "The one who violates," he translated freely and leaned back satisfied by the expected giggle.

He stroked his bald pate and looked archly at the girls.

"The one who violates," he repeated with the pleasure in a platitude of a very old man who has long since forgotten the true nature of titillating vulgarity.

The tittering subsided and there was silence in the room as each waited for the other to make the next move. It was Hope who turned on a small transistor radio and gradually began to move her legs to the rhythm of the hit tune, "Peter Gunn." She was followed by Prudence who rose suddenly and, rooted in the subsoil of the tune, pensively did a few twist movements. The volume was turned up, the music overwhelmed and isolated everyone in the room.

Madam Ritchie looked at her daughters and genuine tears came to her eyes. "Poor Lila," she said. "What a horrible way to die." She brought out a silk hankie but did not use it. "Even if people did spread whatever rumors about her, even if she wasn't as pure as one would wish one's children to be" — and she glanced at her dancing daughters — "even if she did sin in the flesh, even so it was a cruel retribution and she did not deserve it." She flapped the handkerchief to and fro, as if to the rhythm of the music, and as if, too, she were cooling her tears and could not bring herself to the point of removing those signs of her grief. "We all feel threatened, I myself, Hope, Prudence and every girl around here." Her voice grew more intense and the flow of tears diminished, subsided and ceased in a single, large drop that hung on her eyelash. "The evildoer is in our midst! He's on the loose! The monster is among us . . ."

The dresses of the Viking daughters swayed as they jerked into the beat-rhythm. They spun around and around and waggled their whirling behinds at Demosthenes H. de Goede.

"It doesn't matter *who* hears me!" Madam Ritchie raised her voice above the sound of the surrealistic "Peter Gunn." "Even if he is the son of the king. Justice must be done!"

She removed the last tear in a becoming manner with the silk hankie: she dried it and reduced it to a damp little spot on the silk. "We must hide nothing," she said. "We must always be prepared to give the facts," and the sound as she blew her nose was loud above the blare of trumpets.

Then the music ended and Hope and Prudence took up their positions on either side of Detective-Sergeant Demosthenes H. de Goede; and Madam Ritchie folded the handkerchief still smaller, wiped the perspiration from her brow, rolled the handkerchief in the palms of her hands and spirited it between dress and breast where it was pressed damp and firm to strengthen her afresh for the next virtuoso performance.

It was quiet again in the room and suddenly all attention was directed at Detective-Sergeant Demosthenes H. de Goede who, with eyes rigidly fixed on a neutral corner, was apparently sustaining an emotional attack. His respiratory movements were deep and irregular, and he frequently had difficulty in getting his breath back after he had exhaled. Madam Ritchie jerked up straight in her chair, in tow of the emotional results of her innuendoes, deeply impressed by the sensitivity of this perceptive young man, the athletic young god who would protect them against . . . "The Giant!" she said suddenly. "Adam Kadmon Silberstein!"

Although it was a system specially devised by the police college for those who were prevented by their duties from taking part in athletics, it did look ever so much like a state of tension and encouraged her to further loud effusions. "What's the good of concealing it? We all know! The monster! The idiot!"

Detective-Sergeant Demosthenes H. de Goede was busy with isometric exercises for the sake of his stomach muscles . . . You draw in your breath for one count . . . you exhale it for six counts . . .

"There was a mark on Lila's neck!" screamed Madam

Ritchie, carried away. "I saw it myself! Two marks on her throat!"

. . . You force out your stomach when you inhale; you pull it in when you exhale . . .

"A love bite!"

And two sharp little shrieks cut through the room, two shrieks from Hope and Prudence, which were repeated in a duet as they jumped up and looked out through the glass.

Because, for a few seconds, the Giant had appeared and passed the window with clumsy steps.

QUIS? · Chapter Six · Memento
Mori ·· "Life is movement," said Dr.
Johns as they wandered on. "We are never
at a standstill: we are continually on the go." The
earth was wet, the mud clung to their shoes. "Nor is
there any coherence. There are only those fragments that
we encounter on our continual movement and which we wish
to expand into a comprehensible whole." The waters were
noisy in the distant streams and confirmed the complete isolation of everyone who found himself at Welgevonden after
rain. "There is no beginning and no end," said Dr.
Johns.

The blocks, endless blocks, of glass buildings with their
visible residents had suddenly come to an end. The two men
were now ascending a slight rise — a continuation of the lawn
which apparently had no end. For a moment they were
alone on the wide, monotonous landscape and then a group of
figures appeared suddenly over the hump of the rise. They
moved to and fro, like leaves in the wind, and then zigzagged
straight down on Detective-Sergeant Demosthenes H. de
Goede and Dr. Johns: the uncle from Welkom, the uncle from
the Karroo, the aunt with silver hair and the sobbing girl who
looked like a little sow. A group of four, on enormous Welgevonden, looking for relatives.

They shuffled nearer questioningly and Dr. Johns introduced Demosthenes H. de Goede to them. A doctor of medi-
cine and a representative of the law! To them they repre-
sented the pillars of society and they pressed still nearer with
an inundation of questions and reproaches. The uncle from

Welkom raised a hand, subdued them and showed himself
to be in future the leader of the family.

"No," said Dr. Johns. "Lila's mother died at the birth of
her child. Her grandfather, the gardener, and his wife passed
away long ago. She lived by the grace of the owner and
patron of the Foundation, Jock Silberstein. Lila was completely alone and had no living family on Welgevonden."
The uncle from the Karroo looked at the remnants of the
relatives, the last of an unknown generation. He gathered
them in his melancholy gaze as a desolate little group, raised
them proudly to a Gideon's band, ranged them together for all
time. On the great lawn of Welgevonden, on this particular
wet day, a family tie was being forged that, in the future,
would burden the post office with thick letters in blue en-
velopes, with white pages of unformed handwriting that
bemoaned the weather and depicted syndromes with curled
letters that aired grievances and laid claim to blood that was
thicker than water.

"The house where she lived is over there . . ." said Dr.
Johns, and gestured in the direction of an invisible house in
the distance with an asbestos roof.

The uncle from Welkom thanked him on behalf of the
family and restrained himself in time from asking what it
would cost. The thought was simply a matter of habit and a
smile cleaved his lips. This story he simply *had* to tell to his
relatives; perhaps in one of his later letters, when the hurt
had passed. The feeling you had to ask what it cost when
you saw a doctor. And then he suddenly became aware of the
Sergeant.

He called the Sergeant aside and told him the rumor he had heard and, in strict confidence, his own suspicion: that Lila, his niece on his father's side, had been murdered by a giant.

One by one they took their leave of the influential pair and bowed themselves away, the proud citizenry; but not before the old man from Welkom had requested Dr. Johns to thank Jock Silberstein for not having buried their niece in a pauper's coffin.

They moved over the hill as if blown by the slight wind, a group of four on their pilgrimage on behalf of the girl with the white face.

On their way they met the Giant, scattered and regrouped: a united body in silhouette, a corporate body against the horizon. Then they noticed the little house with the asbestos roof in the distance and raised their hands, cheered and disappeared abruptly over the hill.

"It's extraordinary," said Dr. Johns, as at last they left the lawn and wandered along a road, "that all of us at Welgevonden knew Lila's mother. She was eighteen, the girl with the pale face." In the distance they could see a row of cottages surrounded by trees. "One of us was Lila's father, someone here is Lila's brother or sister." Often they had to avoid puddles and turn off to find dry earth between the heather. "And someone slept in unknowing incest with his daughter or sister." Hooting and jeering interrupted his words. They looked around and hastily sought the safety of the heather. "And does that not perhaps reflect a hidden degeneration in

each of us? Lost love, secret sadism, the loved one who becomes hated, animal nature that is made synonymous with
sexuality, the forbidden wish, the longing for revenge because
we have lost paradise?"

Three trucks roared past them, splashed through the mud
and cut deep double tracks in the wet earth. They were all
green and yellow. "Those were the trucks that transported
the wine," said Dr. Johns, "painted with the colors of Welgevonden." At the back of the trucks sat a multitude of people, on benches and caged in by rails, in the manic-depressive
condition of picnickers: a row of faces lifted in maniacal pleasure, with an occasional depressed face in between. "The
quarterly picnic at the trout lake," said Dr. Johns. "Psy-
chotherapeutic recreational joy."

On one side of each of the trucks, in big yellow letters, was
the following legend: THE WELGEVONDEN FOUNDA-
TION; and on the other side, in bilingual resignation: DIE
WELGEVONDEN FONDASIE.

The trucks disappeared over the hill with a lewd skip.

Dr. Johns and Detective-Sergeant Demosthenes H. de
Goede resumed their walk in silence. Detective-Sergeant
Demosthenes H. de Goede was visibly upset by the ravage
caused to his suede shoes by the mud. Presently he asked Dr.
Johns to wait: he removed his shoes, tied the laces together
and hung them around his neck, rolled up his trousers and
resumed his walk, visibly happier.

"Under such circumstances," said Dr. Johns, "it's not at all
surprising that werewolves, succubi, incubi and vampires
haunted people." A single walker appeared around a corner

before them. "But today the fear of our guilty love appears perhaps in other forms." He nodded at the walker. "Or, the worst of all, in ordinary forms."

Reverend Williams greeted these two brothers, whom he had noticed at the funeral, cheerfully.

"Aaaah . . . !" he said, his hand raised, waiting for them to supply their names.

"Doctor Johns . . . Detective-Sergeant Demosthenes H. de Goede," and Dr. Johns gestured with a rapid movement of his hand.

Reverend Williams had been unprepared for the storm. His toilet requisites and clothes were in the city: as he had come, so he was still. The sweat that clung to his under-clothing in the sticky heat, the collar that already showed black marks, the baggy trousers, the saturated shoes heavy with mud, the beard that grew unkempt, brought ruin to the image, based on Billy Graham, of himself as a parson. The approach in tatters belonged to another, folksy, popular, con-vivial type — and in that guise he felt himself strange. There-fore, and not without dignity, he fought the fight, true to him-self, while circumstances entirely beyond his control were systematically stripping him.

Just like the uncle from Welkom, he was instantly tuned in to the wavelength of these quarters.

"A lamentable business," he said and raised his face to a now cloudless heaven. "An extremely unhappy state of affairs," and he turned his gaze on a huge figure standing motion-less in the distance. "Such a lovable child, the victim of an evil world," and he confined his observations to the two

figures before him. "I gather that the whole of Welgevonden
is mourning for this unsullied girl." And suddenly he changed
over to a parsonic diction, in order to maintain his self-esteem
in defiance of the collapse of his personal appearance. He
rocked on his heels as he started his sentences; he rose on his
toes as he reached a period. He hissed his *s*'s and crooned his
n's; he clicked his *c*'s and spat his *t*'s — he orchestrated his
thoughts with the instruments of his words; he passed beyond
the meaning of words, and by means of a combination of tone,
pauses, dashes and resonance of empty rhetoric, he created
Galatea from his hairy fist: a chaste Aphrodite with a white
face, desired and reluctantly ravished; an evil desire of man
aroused by the devil, the original sin in regard to the numen.
The monster as the instrument of Belial!

And then he concluded with an enlightening call from the
clouds for everyone to pass on to performing a glorious deed,
while he sank down on the tips of his toes into the mud.

Entirely renewed, his apparel notwithstanding, he prepared
to leave, but found this beyond the resources of his feeble
physical strength. With the help of Detective-Sergeant Demosthenes H. de Goede he was freed from his shoes, which remained stuck in the mud, and wandered away on tender feet
in resignation across the lovely, soft, yielding earth.

"Your task," said Dr. Johns as they themselves wandered on
slowly in the direction of the cottages, "is heroically great
but not impossible. The Titans and Giants are only remembered because of the battles they lost." He peered at the nearest cottage, which peered back from among a clump of trees.

"It's a legendary fact that evil has always been defeated by the son of a god from a human woman—Hercules, Christ, and . . ." and he nodded approvingly at Detective-Sergeant Demosthenes H. de Goede who, even as they walked, succeeded by means of isometric exercises in massaging his neck muscles, ". . . and also those who are destined by circumstances to become, like Hercules, the champions of the community."

They saw a warning notice beside the road and stopped to look at it.

"Evil is actually impotent," said Dr. Johns. "Satan is the great cuckold of the universe."

It was clear that the notice had been painted by an amateur, although it was strikingly like the danger signals that the Provincial Administration had erected to warn against dangerous conditions which it, under compulsion of rock formation and highway futility, had itself created. Under a red triangle, this particular danger sign begged in shrill yellow letters: THE LORD HAVE MERCY UPON US.

Detective-Sergeant Demosthenes H. de Goede was particularly interested in this phenomenon and took out his notebook in which to write the words. His handwriting, as always, was exceptionally choice and neat.

"Funnily enough," said Dr. Johns as they resumed their walk, "Satan is himself incorporeal. He needs a human being to become visible." They stopped again before another sign. "It's the human being that has become cunning and hidden himself in the struggle."

This notice was coal black and square, with the legend in shining white: WEEPE, FASTE AND PRAYE!

Detective-Sergeant Demosthenes H. de Goede, notebook in hand and pen at the ready, looked questioningly at Dr. Johns.

"Seventeenth-century English," said Dr. Johns. "Circa 1623."

Detective-Sergeant Demosthenes H. de Goede wrote: "Weepe, faste and praye," and right next to that, in brackets, "Weep, fast and pray." He hesitated a moment, then added: "Old E. 1623."

"But perhaps," said Dr. Johns by way of afterthought, as they were drawing close to the cottage, "it is the perfect cunning of Satan. Precisely by resigning himself to his invisibility, now that God is invisible too, he is more difficult to distinguish from God. He is a master planner in the sphere of formlessness, even if he is the ape of God."

The cottage was surrounded by beech trees, narcissus, chincherinchee and daffodils. The road signs had reached a climax in a notice directly in front of the garden gate, where a *Memento Mori* had been placed precisely in the middle of a large board, beneath a wooden cross and a little Virgin figure.

Dr. Johns and Detective-Sergeant Demosthenes H. de Goede stood nearer in order to study the *Memento Mori*.

The central feature was a vertical drawing of an open grave in which a skeleton lay. To left and right were two coffins with corpses in them, each wound in a shroud. In the top left-hand corner the figure of an old man with a long beard leaning on a scythe, with his other hand resting on an hourglass. In the top right-hand corner, a skeleton propped against a skull. Below, in an exact triangle, three death's-heads. Picks and shovels, crossed, balanced the drawing where necessary.

From left to right, at the bottom, was written in black letters:
AND AS I AM, SO MUST YOU BE. THEREFORE PRE-
PARE TO FOLLOW ME.

To one side, at an angle in a corner, in cursive letters, the
creator of the *Memento* (and, in fact, of the danger signs also)
was given: *"O'Hara pinxit."*

Detective-Sergeant Demosthenes H. de Goede had already
taken out his notebook and set aside a blank page when Dr.
Johns stopped him and drew his attention to a small shelf next
to the notice where a whole pile of these pamphlets was available. Each took one and then went through the garden gate.

They admired the daffodils and the chincherinchee and the
beds full of flowers that shone fresh and colorful in the sunlight. Then they noticed another small notice, hidden among
the flora, hardly three inches above the ground: A WET
SPRING RAISES FEAR OF FAMINE.

The door of the cottage was painted red and Dr. Johns was
about to knock when he saw an illuminated manuscript, beautifully designed in many colors, and fastened with drawing
pins to the wall beside the doorframe. He put on his glasses
and studied the notice attentively.

"Amazing!" he said to Demosthenes H. de Goede. "Something one seldom sees: a genuine Bill of Mortality." He took
off his glasses and returned them to his pocket. "I think they
first appeared in the days of Louis XIV, but this one is considerably different and shows a good deal of English influence." He beckoned to Detective-Sergeant de Goede to come
nearer. "As you'll notice, there are three columns: the name
in the first column, the day of death in the second, and the

cause of death in the third." He glanced fleetingly through the names. "Very, very interesting," he said. "Here is the history of old residents and of regular visitors to Welgevonden."

Detective-Sergeant Demosthenes H. de Goede read the names and made brief notes on cause of death:

NAME	CAUSE OF DEATH
Old Mrs. Silberstein ("The Duchess")	Liver growne
Sir Henry Mandrake	Plannett strucke
Miss Agatha Silberstein	Aged
Miss Florence Silberstein	Aged
The "Gardener"	King's Evill
Giepie Ollenwaar	Gored by a bull
J. J. van Eeden	Infection by germ *Spirochaeta pallida*
Bebe Gulbenkian	Throwne by horse
20 Unknowne Blacks	In course of disturbances
One Albino Baby	Shot
Salome Silberstein	At birthe of monstrous childe

Detective-Sergeant Demosthenes H. de Goede found that his notebook was getting full and contented himself with looking quickly through the remaining names. He wrote the last name of all down, however.

Lila	Murthered by a Giant

After Dr. Johns had knocked at the door, he
stood back and looked closely at the window beside
it. Meanwhile, Detective-Sergeant Demosthenes H. de
Goede busied himself with putting on his shoes, combing his
hair and tidying himself up in various ways after the exacting
walk through the mud.

"He suffers from senile decay," said Dr. Johns, "but during
a *lucidum intervallum* he remains one of my best friends. If
he scrabbles at the windowpane in order to get out, we shall
have to postpone the visit until later."

They both now looked at the window. After a while they
heard footsteps and the curtains were drawn aside. A small
face, wizened with age, dwarfed by a broad-brimmed hat,
peered somberly through the pane. A staff was held in a bony
white hand and a large toga hung overbearingly across meager
shoulders: the apparel of a funeral bearer at the time of the
Great Plague. He was completely passive.

"Thank God, he's normal," said Dr. Johns. "We can go in."

He produced a key and unlocked the door. The sad little
figure appeared full-length in the doorway and held out his
hand to Dr. Johns. Dr. Johns handed over a key, and he seized
it eagerly. The toga hung to his feet and swayed to and fro
as he fumbled to find the pocket among all the folds. Only
when he had pocketed the key, and placed the staff against a
wall, did he come outside; and then he underwent a complete
transformation. A toothless smile split his face, his small eyes
narrowed and sparkled with alertness. He embraced Dr.

Johns and then turned to Detective-Sergeant Demosthenes
H. de Goede, waiting courteously to be introduced to him.

"Judge O'Hara," said Dr. Johns. "Detective-Sergeant Demosthenes H. de Goede."

Judge O'Hara nodded amiably, and Detective-Sergeant
Demosthenes H. de Goede, instantly adjusted to the demands
of propriety of the jurisprudential hierarchy, saluted smartly:
for the rest of the meeting, alert and in his proper place, he
would observe protocol.

They were led into a small inside room, which the sunlight,
falling through barred windows, lighted and showed to contain leather-covered chairs and book-filled shelves which
created the impression of an exclusive club in colonial days.

"I presume I may keep the key?" said Judge O'Hara to Dr.
Johns, as he poured them each a whisky and soda. The Sergeant was given a beer.

"But certainly, my good friend," said Dr. Johns.

"It's not that I find the isolation unwholesome," said Judge
O'Hara, and raised his glass to Demosthenes H. de Goede. "It's
simply the fact that I have a good deal of work to do and that
my activities are not confined to the room."

They drank in silence and Judge O'Hara folded the toga
over his knees and settled the medieval hat more comfortably
on his head.

"Detective-Sergeant Demosthenes H. de Goede is here in
connection with the investigation into the death of Lila," said
Dr. Johns.

For a moment the name meant nothing to Judge O'Hara,
and Dr. Johns explained who she was: the daughter of the

white-faced girl, the granddaughter of the gardener who lived in the cottage with the asbestos roof, the white-faced girl who died at the birth of her daughter, Lila, who had just been murdered by an unknown sadist.

"Naturally," said Judge O'Hara. "The one who was raped by a Giant. I remember her well" — and he placed the tips of his fingers together in a judicial gesture. "I assume you have already arrested the miscreant, Sergeant." He turned to Demosthenes H. de Goede, who began to stutter diligently, but Dr. Johns interrupted and explained that Detective-Sergeant Demosthenes H. de Goede was, at this stage, merely getting acquainted with the residents of Welgevonden.

"The rape or dishonoring of a virgin has been one of the greatest sins since the earliest times," said Judge O'Hara, and poured himself and Dr. Johns another whisky and soda. "Among the Jews the corrupter of the maiden had, for instance, to pay *zohar* to her father." He nodded with approval when Detective-Sergeant Demosthenes H. de Goede refused a second beer. "At the time of Moses, a man who deflowered a maiden was stoned." The hat was too low over his eyes and he shifted it higher up, but a moment later it was back over his eyes. "I have read," said Judge O'Hara, "that the basis for this singular retribution was the fear of demoniacal powers. Sexuality is the territory of evil, and the protected maidenly opening can only be made use of under the protection of a magical counterritual." He offered Dr. Johns a third drink, which was not refused. He himself took a couple of long sips and relaxed, a genial medieval funeral bearer in his toga, which enclosed him in his chair like a big black blanket. "The chief method of exorcism was to kick up a noise during coitus and thus to drive the evil spirits away. It is said that Rabbi Ben Huna rang a bell in such circumstances."

Both he and Dr. Johns shook peacefully in a fit of lively laughter while Detective-Sergeant Demosthenes H. de Goede kept his eyes high-mindedly, and his mind attentively, on the Judge.

"And then there are still the magical powers of purification of water," Judge O'Hara continued. "The Talmud calls fresh rainwater . . ."

"Adam Kadmon Silberstein, for instance, takes a regular bath near the masks, every morning," said Dr. Johns, and looked meaningfully at Detective-Sergeant Demosthenes H. de Goede.

"And fire," said Judge O'Hara. "The burning sconce . . ."

"And amulets," added Dr. Johns.

"Amulets," said Judge O'Hara, "in the form of sexual symbols. At the mysteries of Eleusis the pudenda was the vulva; the crown of the Emperor of Kafa was a phallic triangle." He turned to Detective-Sergeant Demosthenes H. de Goede. "Do you, for example, know the sign of the fig in Italy to protect oneself against the *malocchio?*"

Detective-Sergeant Demosthenes H. de Goede strained his memory to the utmost: his search covered the entire field of General Knowledge, Cultural Studies, Strange Customs to Some Aspects of Cosmology, as he had learned them in his final year at the police college, but he declared himself stutteringly defeated by the Judge's greater learning.

Judge O'Hara illustrated for him the sign of the vulva, **and**

Detective-Sergeant Demosthenes H. de Goede went red to behind his ears when he recognized the indecent gesture of his childhood.

"But to return to serious matters," said Judge O'Hara, after he had refilled the two glasses, "the fury of the community is unleashed fully when the maiden, actually its protection against evil, is deflowered. And I imagine that you, in your perambulation of the estate, have been struck by this atmosphere of revenge . . ."

He looked questioningly at his two guests.

"We have still to determine if Lila was raped," said Dr. Johns carefully. "Detective-Sergeant Demosthenes H. de Goede and I have even considered whether we shall perhaps not have to exhume the deceased."

Suddenly Judge O'Hara sat up straight in his chair. The perpetual sparkle disappeared from his eyes, the depression of a while back returned to him.

"Exactly! Exactly . . ." he began, and stood up in confusion. The folds of the toga fell over his feet, the small figure became ominous in his strange apparel.

"And I know what you will find," said Judge O'Hara in a sepulchral voice. "Warm blood in her breasts and *in fundo ventricoli* . . . her face flushed, her limbs soft and supple . . . her hair and nails long and overgrown . . . her lips, cheeks and breasts swollen with fresh blood . . . new blood pulsing *in ventricolo cordis* . . ."

He walked tensely to and fro, obsessed by the image.

Dr. Johns stood up and beckoned to Detective-Sergeant Demosthenes H. de Goede.

"Make a cross of tar on every door tonight!" said Judge

O'Hara and seized Dr. Johns by the arm. "Invoke Saint Rochus, and Saint Sebastian and Saint Adrian to protect you." He pulled Detective-Sergeant Demosthenes H. de Goede nearer, too, in the iron grip of his bony hands. "Beware of the confidant who will come in false form!"

"We will disinter her," said Dr. Johns placatingly, "simply to determine the true nature of her death, and Detective-Sergeant Demosthenes H. de Goede will do the necessary."

"Destroy the bloodthirsty friend of Samchasai!" called Judge O'Hara and seized his staff.

Dr. Johns pointed, unobserved, to the door and he and Detective-Sergeant Demosthenes H. de Goede began to move slowly toward it.

"Carry the sacred relics with you constantly! Never be without the Pascal wax! Write out the first fourteen verses of Saint John and never be without them! Wear the medal of Saint Benedict! Sing a requiem over the grave!" He opened his toga and revealed an undergarment which had scoured his sensitive skin until it was blood red. "Chastise yourself with the hair of the Cilician goat!"

Dr. Johns and the Detective were already at the door, but Judge O'Hara barred their way, his small eyes glowing with inner fire.

"I saw his sharp, long teeth! He assaults men, women and children! He uses the body to renew himself! He does not spare even his own sister!"

Dr. Johns and Detective-Sergeant Demosthenes H. de Goede slipped through the door and looked back at Judge O'Hara standing with his staff aloft.

"Strew garlic on her grave! Destroy the pernicious incubus

with the pale face and the red hair! They're the hallmarks of the Pamgri!"

He came toward them, flecks of foam at the corners of his mouth.

"Drive a wooden spike through her heart, because the curse is upon her! Transfix her with wood for the peace of her eternal soul!"

Dr. Johns slammed the door on him and, when he tried to get out, locked it with another key.

"His key was a dummy," said Dr. Johns as they left. "I make sure before I give him the right key," and he looked sadly back at the little black figure who, scrabbling at the window, was trying vainly to get out.

QUIS? · Chapter Eight · The Descendants of Brutus the Bull ·· "Perhaps at this stage I should tell you more about the Foundation," said Dr. Johns as he and Detective-Sergeant Demosthenes H. de Goede walked away from the cottage in the direction of the farming area and the huge buildings in the distance known as the factory, the bottling plant and the cellars. They climbed a hill and wandered through paddocks in which sheep of various breeds were peacefully feeding on alfalfa and were so fat from little exercise and abundant food that they could hardly move. Around each paddock there was gathered a small group of people, where men in white were giving lectures.

"Around you," said Dr. Johns, "you will see visitors, as well as residents and members of the family. Residents are allowed to have their families with them and it often happens that the residents, together with their families, decide to stay on even when they have received their discharge." He smiled at Demosthenes H. de Goede, who kept looking back at the cottage they had just left. "We are also often overwhelmed by visitors from outside and there are an unusual number of them now, because of a special occasion." He listened to the waters thundering through the masks. "At the moment, everyone has been trapped by the streams, and that naturally simplifies your task. I mean, it's like a detective story: the ideal seclusion, the broken communications, the castle in the forest, the disrupted paradise."

Detective-Sergeant Demosthenes H. de Goede stammered a question and Dr. Johns listened carefully.

"The special occasion?" His face cleared and he himself became excited. "A particularly important event, and I trust that you will do everything in your power to prevent the unfortunate recent incident and the bitter task that lies ahead from harming the proceedings." He waited until he had received Detective-Sergeant Demosthenes H. de Goede's gesture of promise. "Good! D'you see, the authorities concerned, which sanction the Foundation and contribute to it, rand for rand, have seen fit to make an award to Jock Silberstein and two others. The dignitaries, properly trapped . . ." He laughed delightedly at his own joke. "The trapped dignitaries are already here, and the award will be made at a function tomorrow evening. We hope to have a full house and we hope that, by that time, the unpleasant task will have been accomplished." He was silent for a while. "Speed is therefore a necessity."

Detective-Sergeant Demosthenes H. de Goede increased his pace impulsively and Dr. Johns, with his short steps, had difficulty in keeping up. He was, however, remarkably athletic for someone of his advanced age.

"It is felt, however," Dr. Johns continued, "that a doctorate cannot be dished out too lightly, especially because more than one person attached to the Foundation is concerned, so accordingly only Jock Silberstein will receive a doctor's degree, *honoris causa*, and the others suitable lesser degrees."

They had already left the loafing yards and were on their way to a farther group of people gathered around cattle in a paddock.

"The second person is Henry Silberstein-van Eeden, Jock

Silberstein's son-in-law . . . And, may I add, certainly the hardest worker and the axis around which everything in this organization revolves. He deserves the degree of M.A. Admin., *honoris causa*." Dr. Johns was slightly winded in his attempt to keep up with Detective-Sergeant Demosthenes H. de Goede, who had unwittingly warmed up to racing speed.

Detective-Sergeant Demosthenes H. de Goede had often taken part in walking races at the police college and he unconsciously applied the necessary movements to attain the maximum speed: his elbows raised high, his shoulders hunched, his fists just grazing his chin, like pistons, and his legs moving in that singular movement that only the connoisseur can distinguish from a trot.

"The other person is Giepie Ollenwaar, the founder of the red-black Ollenwaar Stud Association."

Dr. Johns was now *trotting* unashamedly.

"M.Sc. Agric., *honoris causa*," he gasped.

At that speed they approached the crowd around the cattle with unnecessary haste and then suddenly came to a halt, both breathing deeply.

"Uncle Giepie Ollenwaar, of blessed memory," said Dr. Johns, "died eighteen years ago, however; but the authorities have seen fit to bestow the degree on him *in absentia*, because of his exceptional contribution."

Detective-Sergeant Demosthenes H. de Goede had immediately made use of his faster breathing and employed it for isometric application. (You merely extend your stomach and then draw it in against the movement of normal breathing. It's also excellent for the lungs.)

They now walked more sedately toward the circle of people who, greeting him, made room for Dr. Johns. A man in a white overall was about to speak.

"That's Dries van Schalkwyk," whispered Dr. Johns, "the well-beloved secretary of the association and also a special field officer of the Foundation."

A well-built, sunburned man with bristle-brush hair going gray in neat speckles at the temples, laughed at the crowd with a strong row of false teeth. A small, skinny bull with a curiously patterned skin color was snuffling at him in a friendly way, and he repeatedly repulsed the shy muzzle with his elbow.

"Dear friends," began Dries van Schalkwyk; and then he spotted Dr. Johns. He rubbed his hands together. "Dear friends, we have the special honor . . ." — and he came down from his dais — ". . . to have . . ." — he took Dr. Johns by the arm and exhibited him — "Doctor Johns in our midst." He waited for the applause, which came only from the residents of Welgevonden; relatives and visitors stood aloof, watching.

Dr. Johns whispered something in his ear.

"And, friends," he said, "an exceptional honor." He took Demosthenes de Goede by the arm, too, and conducted both of them over the rope around the ring, up to the dais and the interested bull. "Detective-Sergeant Demosthenes H. de Goede!"

There was a ripple through the audience and heads bumped together knowingly in whispers that presently changed to thunderous applause. It lasted a full minute, and Detective-

Sergeant Demosthenes H. de Goede, encouraged by the well-beloved Dries, was obliged (against police regulations) to mount the dais. He was a magnificent man, and towered athletically above everyone: modest, mute and reassuring. He raised his fists in a boxer's gesture, dropped his head modestly to receive their adulation. At the right moment, with a sense of timing peculiar to the hero, he retired and allowed the speaker to continue with the proceedings.

"Dear friends," said Dries van Schalkwyk, "our time is limited," and he looked down at his precious wristwatch, and then up again, with an unexpected change of emotion to seriousness and devotion which only the deceptive fool of understanding can handle. "It is a habit I have followed without apology for eighteen years, and will repeat in the future." He glared proudly and challengingly at the invisible scoffer on the horizon. "Each year I ask those present to observe a moment's silence in honor of the death and memory of Uncle Giepie."

It was the residents and their relations who first fell silent, and then the visitors who followed their example and made the silence moving. Even the wind lay still. It was an all-embracing silence that descended on the Foundation, and brought them nearer the earth and nature. Only the masks were noisy, and emphasized the inner conflict. Then the well-beloved Dries raised his hand and began his address.

"Dear friends, it isn't necessary for me to tell the residents and friends of Welgevonden who Uncle Giepie was and what he accomplished, but" — and he looked searchingly at the unknown faces — "on account of the visitors and dignitaries in our midst, I should like to say a little about that remarkable man." He cleared his throat, bared his teeth and rolled his eyes back, back into his thoughts where history was engraved.

"Thirty-six years ago a poor field worker like myself . . . (giggling) . . . took a look at the whole of the breeding position and decided that he would, with the scanty means at his disposal, take the bull by the horns . . . (appreciative laughter) . . . and follow his own breeding principles. He began with one bull . . . (he held up his forefinger) . . . and with two cows . . . (here he held up two fingers). Imagine to yourselves: one bull and two cows." He paused for dramatic effect. "That same poor son of the countryside, eighteen years later, left THREE HUNDRED THOUSAND RAND to the Welgevonden Foundation." The anticipated murmur that, every year, ran through the audience, ran through it again now. The well-beloved Dries listened to it with a touch of nostalgia and the bitter cynicism of a priest who, later, would have to curb the enthusiastic abandon of new converts. He took a sip of water and looked at the dignitaries who were nodding approvingly at one another. (Someone began to clap hands, but stopped immediately, as the well-beloved Dries remained silent and smiled forgivingly.) "That same Giepie Ollenwaar, who will be remembered not only for the three hundred thousand rand, but for a gift made one evening to a young couple, a gift that cannot be judged by money, a lovely event one summer evening at Welgevonden . . ." He allowed a silence to establish itself, then broke it. "A gift of the legendary bull, the mighty Brutus, to Henry and Salome Silberstein."

He had complete control of his audience and looked at them with proud deprecation. The skinny little bull in the arena had come closer and was snuffling carefully at him with his wet muzzle. The well-beloved Dries stroked him absent-mindedly between his ears and patted him away.

"Dear friends," said Dries in rising tones and genuine abandon, "Giepie Ollenwaar was eighteen years ahead of his time, but he was a man who at his death did not hesitate to say . . . to me, that unforgettable evening . . . 'Improve on Brutus, Dries. Do not let the breeding policy die with me!' "

Beloved Dries had suddenly become white and calm and quiet — that dangerous calm of the dedicated, that silence in which lies power. He raised his face to the horizon where a giant-like figure appeared and then he lowered his unseeing gaze to the faces before him.

"And it was then, dear friends, that I realized that Uncle Giepie meant more than the indifferent, materialistic, conservative, right-wing reactionary would understand. I humbly, friends, accepted the mantle of Elia."

The residents lived every moment, the ordinary visitors were in the dark and yet in a rapture, the eminent visitors inquired from their guide the name of the official.

The well-beloved Dries now spoke faster, more carelessly — almost self-deprecatingly.

"I accepted a task, friends, and carried on. Brutus was not the end. I kept pace with the times. I interpreted the prophetic thought of Uncle Giepie to the best of my ability. At the very outset I asked myself: does the world really want great and mighty stud bulls? Does it accord with the Will of our People? Do they not eat too much? Are they not uncontrollable? Do they meet the requirements of the Ordinary Breeder?" He was silent for a moment. "Those, friends, were all questions that I asked myself in the silence of my room. And then" — he brought his hands together — "and then, friends, I asked myself the following question: those great horns of Brutus . . . does one sell horns to the abattoirs? Does the meat attain to the desired grade if the animals have bashed each other in the trucks with those great horns?" He raised his hands pensively to his head. "And I asked myself, seeing Brutus there, with the black and the red, the two colors so strongly segregated . . . so definitely and challengingly apart: what psychological effect would that have on the buyer?" He lowered his hands. "It was very far from being my intention to yield . . . but I asked myself: who is the buyer? How sensitively attuned is he, aesthetically, to the question of color? And I immediately realized, friends, that adaptability was the answer. Not cunning in regard to the quality of your product, but to give as little offense as possible, to eliminate the petty, simply to feed the peoples and to satisfy the demands of a steadily increasing world population."

There was applause from the eminent visitors; and the inhabitants, family and friends, although somewhat in the dark as far as this new trend in Dries' annual speech was concerned, joined in boisterously.

"Then I decided, friends . . ." (his shirttail had come out of his pants and he tucked it back) . . . "my shirt's hanging out, friends . . . then I decided to shift the colors to a horizontal basis: the black above, the red below, except, and this is important, around the genitals, for manifestly scientific reasons."

He took a sip of water and then saw for the first time the lumpish figure of the Giant slowly approaching the assembly. He frowned and took another sip.

"And now, friends, my time is limited — certain technical considerations." He brought out a piece of paper and consulted it swiftly. He suppressed a smile and put the paper back in the pocket of his jacket. "As you know, friends, breeding power comes above all. It's not what a bull looks like, but how he breeds. It is not only *that* he breeds, but when he breeds." He smiled audaciously at his audience. "We are all scientists here; the ladies will excuse us." He took from his pocket a hen's egg and looked attentively at it, then hid it in the hollow of his hand. "You probably know about Pavlov's experiments, friends . . ." A single individual in the audience nodded. Dries pointed. ". . . a friend, there. But perhaps I should explain." He closed his eyes. "I took one of Brutus' children, a young bull, and brought him to the heifers. Once we had shown him a circular object, we allowed him to cover the heifers. Once we had shown him a square object, we gave him an electric shock." He opened his eyes. "By repetition, friends, the pattern was established and he covered the heifers only when he had seen the circular object. And then we progressed to the next step." He looked at the egg in his hand, then folded it away again. "Then, friends, then we showed the young bull an oval-shaped object — not a circle and not a square. And what was the result?" The solitary individual, who knew, leaned back comfortably and whispered something to his neighbor. "Then, friends, this little bull had a real nervous breakdown because of his inability to come to a decision in the direction in which he had been conditioned."

The well-beloved Dries descended suddenly from the dais and looked lovingly at the skinny little bull that had all the time been snuffling him. Then he looked at the gathering.

"The time has come, friends, to illustrate."

He raised his hand, the fist balled. The little bull looked at it eagerly with its warm, soft eyes. He opened his fist and revealed the egg, held between thumb and forefinger. The bullock staggered back, its eyes became glazed, it lowed sonorously in pain, slowly its legs gave way and it collapsed. The well-beloved Dries mounted the rostrum again and waited smilingly for the tumult to die down. He offered the egg courteously to one of the women, wiped his hands on a handkerchief and took a sip of water. Meanwhile, the bullock lay peacefully on the ground, as if in a state of total hypnosis.

"Now, friends," said the well-beloved Dries. "You have probably seen the application long ago. Through a method of selection and mating we have determined these characteristics in the descendants of Brutus and have thereby managed, in the words of the amateur, to establish, as it were, a sort of built-in birth control."

Apart from the residents and relations who understood the breeding policy, the rest of the audience seemed altogether mystified and the well-beloved Dries smiled forgivingly.

"Perhaps I should explain further," he said and winked at one of the older residents who was bubbling with excitement and threatening to stand up and himself explain.

The well-beloved Dries raised his hand slightly, subdued the older inhabitant and resumed.

"One would like the heifers to be covered when conditions are ideal and when the heifers . . ." He looked questioningly at the audience.

"Are fat!" shouted the older resident.

"And," said Dries, "and when the heifers are fat, the genital periphery . . ."

He waited in vain.

"When the heifers are fat we say they are what from fatness . . ."

"Round," shouted the older resident and suddenly the audience grasped Dries' thought process. Great excitement ensued and they could hardly wait for him to continue.

"And when it's been a dry year and the heifers are skinny and everything hangs, then the form is no longer round but . . ."

"Square," said one of the eminent visitors inadvertently.

Dries shook his head benignly.

"That's impossible," he said. "When everything hangs the shape is . . ."

"Oval!" bawled the older resident and looked contemptuously at the eminent guest who tried in vain to conceal his discomfort.

"And when the shape is oval," said Dries, "then . . ." and he pointed significantly at the little bull, which still lay in schizophrenic inertia.

At that moment the Giant appeared among them and forced his way genially up to the bullock. He towered huge above the people, who unconsciously made way for him and looked at him apprehensively. The Giant kicked the animal gently and at this touch it began to show life at once, regained its legs and began snuffling the Giant.

Dries' smile had vanished, but he took no notice of the Giant. He ignored him as a speaker ignores a troublesome heckler at a meeting.

"At the slightest touch the bull recovered," he said. "In times of plenty the heifers are covered; in times of scarcity they are not covered. That, friends, was my breeding policy and on it I have built."

The attention of the audience was clearly no longer entirely with the speaker. They were entranced by the spectacle of the Giant and the little bull, which looked like a pet beside him. They were all discussing the sight with each other, except the older resident who had shifted up to the eminent visitor and was trying to gain his attention.

"Dear friends . . . order, friends! Friends, that was therefore the breeding policy laid down, and it is my proud privilege hereby to announce that this year I can display Brutus III to you."

It should have been a great moment, but something had gone wrong.

The older resident had managed to catch the attention of the eminent visitor, and snarled at him: "Cobbler, stick to your last." Then, satisfied, he shuffled back to his place.

The well-beloved Dries grimaced and raised his voice. (This was the breeder's lot; even Uncle Giepie had had, many a day, to tolerate the Philistinism of people.)

"Dear friends, whereas Brutus was a colossal, clumsy animal, we have here a smaller animal, perfectly proportioned."

He paused and drank deeply from the glass of water. "Whereas Brutus was voiceless, this animal has a beautiful deep voice: a sign of normal development." He hesitated, for this was the moment at which he had intended to make his joke: one bull, one voice. He decided against it. "Whereas Brutus had a fierce character and a wild nature, and killed even his creator . . ." Ah, he had their attention again. Their conversation ceased and they listened again. But he would punish them and not refer to the matter again. "Whereas Brutus was destructive, this animal is by nature gentle and even tempered." He had once again lost the attention of the audience. "Whereas this animal caused no losses at mating time, Brutus injured and overpowered the heifers." He deliberately did not look at the Giant. He looked at his watch and decided suddenly to stop. He had retrieved their attention, but had lost his own enthusiasm. This year, the year of his triumph before so many eminent guests, something had gone awry. He suppressed with difficulty his fury toward the Giant.

"A few final announcements before we separate, friends," he said. "I remind you of tomorrow evening's proceedings, when certain awards will be made to Mr. Jock Silberstein, Mr. Henry Silberstein-van Eeden, and to Uncle Giepie Ollenwaar, *in absentia*. A full attendance will be appreciated. And lastly, I request you to pause for a moment in silent meditation in memory of our beloved Lila who was recently so brutally murdered."

This time he looked straight at the Giant as the audience fell silent and the masks began to roar.

Thereafter the well-beloved Dries took up his satchel and

walked rapidly toward his room, followed by the playfully gamboling little bull without horns. His figure had suddenly sagged, as if all the cares in the world were on his shoulders. He had been overcome with listlessness. He had lost his enthusiasm, and in the world of breeding that was fatal. Once you begin to doubt your calling, then the muse in you dies. The murderer had killed not only Lila, but something bigger. Tears began to trickle down his cheeks. This cried out to Heaven for retribution!

Residents, relations, guests and prominent visitors had left in groups the place where the universally-liked Dries had so unexpectedly concluded his address. African helpers had already removed the ring, the dais and the remaining cattle. The proceedings had been shortened by at least an hour and the entire program had been spoiled. One of the guides tried to regroup everyone and fill out their hour with the last part of a lecture on German merino sheep. It would mean that this group's time would end with the first half of a lecture about something else — but that could not be helped.

"You'll notice," said Dr. Johns to Detective-Sergeant Demosthenes H. de Goede, as they went on, "that here the emphasis is placed on farming and farming methods. But that was one of Jock Silberstein's conditions for the grant and the establishment of the Foundation." He sniffed the fresh air and exhaled it pleasurably. "It's a back-to-the-soil policy, a theory that there is a magical quality, a healing property, associated with everything to do with farming. It's a cult to which you expose yourself — so widespread that it reaches any group level of intelligence or development. It's actually the experience of a myth."

He peered over his shoulder and pointed out to Detective-Sergeant Demosthenes H. de Goede that the Giant was following them.

"The theory is," said Dr. Johns, "that in the cycles of nature all psychic material is realized, that the psychic processes

are given form here. Welgevonden is teeming with primordial images — and the residents are encouraged to determine their spiritual coherence by personal experience."

They now approached a shining aluminum tank, held in
position eighty feet into the air by four standards. A vertical
ladder connected the ground with an observation tower up
above. Dr. Johns indicated to Detective-Sergeant Demosthenes H. de Goede that he should lead, and he did so dexterously,
like a naval cadet. Halfway up he swung out into the thin air
and waved his hat exuberantly. He did the rest of the distance
in record time and relaxed in isometric repose while waiting
for Dr. Johns to follow him.

The little, bald-headed old man climbed considerably more
slowly and laboriously. He turned first red then blue from
exertion and reached the platform in a state of complete ex-
haustion. He recovered slowly and peacefully and then introduced Detective-Sergeant Demosthenes H. de Goede to
someone who had watched their arrival from the farthermost
point of the platform and who now came forward to meet
them.

He was an attractive middle-aged man of steady, efficient
appearance. He was dressed neatly in the livery of a rich
farmer: suede shoes, a well-cut pair of khaki trousers, a Harris
tweed jacket and a cravat which protruded just above his silk
shirt. He was sunburned and his hair had been cut by an Italian
barber. Sunglasses obscured his eyes, but the smile with which
he greeted them was frank and sincere. He thrust out a farmer's hand to Detective-Sergeant Demosthenes H. de Goede,
who reciprocated the iron grip with one of steel.

"Mr. Silberstein-van Eeden . . . Detective-Sergeant Demosthenes H. de Goede," said Dr. Johns.

Shortly after this introduction, the platform jerked beneath
the pressure of a further weight, and the Giant appeared. It
was as if everything had suddenly become smaller: the tank,
the platform, the entire structure. It seemed at times that the
Giant would lose his balance at any moment and tumble
down, but he came safely nearer, waveringly, and sat down
next to Henry Silberstein-van Eeden. He fumbled along
Henry's side until he found his hand and folded it firmly in
his own. The parody of father and son on that swaying platform — the monster and the solid citizen, the expansive landscape, the isolation high in the thin blue air — was fixed for
a moment like a photograph in Dr. Johns' mind, and he cried
out involuntarily: *"Riboine-sjeloilom: kuk arop fun dem himl
un kuk dir on dayn velt!"* (Dear Lord: look down from your
heaven and see what is happening to your world.)

Beneath them the empty tank glowed in the sun and
bounced beams of light against their eyes. The echo of every
movement roared back. The evasive odor of grapes still clung
to the sides; and below them, as far as they could see, stretched
the Welgevonden estate, gleaming back from a thousand windows. The residents, relatives, visitors and distinguished guests
moved like ants through the Foundation.

There was a clattering on the ladder: small metal sounds
that announced a new arrival. Reverend Williams rose, tattered, up through the thin air and walked with burning feet
across the hot iron to them, his jacket crumpled, his collar
dirty, his beard misleadingly masculine. He nodded five times

in a circle, breathed the air in and was transported by the landscape, nature all unspoiled. He saw the crude earth, the virgin,
the Lila-image, and then he sharpened his gaze and noticed the
glittering of glass and all the movement, and he called out a
curse on all forms of violation.

"God forgive you," he said to the Giant, who sought sanctuary beside his father.

The platform rang beneath the onslaught of many feet on
rungs that made the ladder sound like a scale. Residents, relatives, guests and visitors poured up and across the platform
and milled together ever more tightly in a circle that quickly
became compressed into immobility. The distracted guide
clung to the ladder and bellowed out his comment on the
sights worth seeing to the clouds. He described all they could
see in smooth-worn adjectives and encouraged them to spurt
out a fountain of admiring Ooo's and Ah's. Then he invited
them to spit, to see if they could reach the ground, until their
saliva, carried on the wind, became a misty rain that never
reached the ground but disintegrated in the air. He asked them
to shout so that they could hear the echoes against the mountain, and their collective voices tore up the ravines, echoed
from the cliffs and disappeared in a lament over the abysses.
He asked them to be silent so that they could hear the masks
and, in the silence, they heard them. Then he asked them to
cheer and to express their delight in free nature. And beneath
the cheering, as everyone cast his *doppelgänger* over the preci-
pice, there rose into the sky an article of clothing, which filled
with wind, stretched puffed-out arms in a gesture of benedic-
tion over the earth, and drifted slowly above the Foundation.
Then the circle was complete and they were sucked back

through the loudspeaker and chivied down again until only the Giant, his father, the Detective-Sergeant and Dr. Johns remained with Reverend Williams who, after the ecstatic exuberance of a moment ago, found himself without his jacket.

He, too, departed: hopping across the hot metal, skipping lightly down the ladder until he appeared again down below, his hands before his eyes, his face raised to the drifting garment that, specklike, disappeared over the horizon.

Henry Silberstein-van Eeden, his son hanging lovingly on his arm, turned to Dr. Johns and Detective-Sergeant Demosthenes H. de Goede.

"Do you remember our conversations, Doctor Johns? How you and Judge O'Hara, eighteen years ago, patiently led me to a conception of the nature of chaos and order?"

He endured the fawning adulation of the Giant without any outward sign of feeling. He allowed the Giant to place his heavy arm around his shoulders and to press himself loutishly against him.

"Doctor Johns and Judge O'Hara were my mentors," said Henry Silberstein-van Eeden to Detective-Sergeant Demosthenes H. de Goede. And then to Dr. Johns: "Aren't you proud of your product?" And a little later: "And how's our friend getting on?"

"He was not allowed the key today," said Dr. Johns. "The murder, alas, upset him."

Henry Silberstein-van Eeden nodded understandingly. He sighed and shook the Giant's left arm from his shoulder.

"It's strange that no sooner did I see the beauty of order, than my mentor should have become involved in the struggle. Did order overwhelm him, Doctor Johns?"

"Chaos," said Dr. Johns.

Henry was powerless in the grip of a sentimental embrace.

"I am completely adapted," said Henry, "and I understand my emotions." He tried in vain to wriggle free. "I hate and I feel no guilt. You taught me everything . . . love of order and for Salome, who was part of it. Do you remember her still after eighteen years, Doctor Johns? She was part of Welgevonden. When I married her I became part of it, too. She was the crown that you spread over everything." Unexpectedly he wriggled free. "I had truly not had enough of her, and just when I reached the stage of nearly understanding everything, she died. Have I not the right to hate?" — and once again he was smothered under another embrace.

Dr. Johns placed his hand warningly on Demosthenes H. de Goede who, like a coiled spring, might come swiftly uncoiled at any moment. Detective-Sergeant Demosthenes H. de Goede relaxed gradually and moved to the edge of the platform from where he looked out over the Foundation and, with bulging abdominal muscles, combined countertension and isometric exercises almost motionlessly in his warming up for the struggle that lay certainly ahead.

"Why must I accept fate that determines everything blindly? Have I not the fullest right to revolt, although I can do nothing about it?"

Henry Silberstein-van Eeden, smothered by love, could hardly articulate his last sentence.

"She was dead before I understood everything," said Henry. "The struggle between chaos and order is the struggle between chaos and the Welgevonden in which Salome's spirit is embodied." His voice was inaudible under the embrace.

"As a father I utter my curse . . ." His words were muted, for in a moment of uncontrolled abandon the Giant kissed his father full on the mouth. ". . . Utter my curse," repeated Henry, half stupefied, just before Dr. Johns struck the Giant away and sent him stumbling to the edge of the platform. "I expressed my curse," said Henry, "upon the one who threatens order, upon a brother who murdered his sister."

Dumbfounded, the Giant walked around them to the ladder. He looked at them and began slowly to climb down. His feet struck deep sounds from each rung, his huge body disappeared gradually until only his white face and red hair protruded, disembodied, over the rim of the platform. His blue eyes remained sadly on Henry.

"Because, you know, Doctor Johns," said Henry, "she could have been the sister . . ."

"Or the daughter . . ." said Dr. Johns.

". . . of any one of us," said Henry.

They both reflected deeply and then Henry said: "Do you know, Doctor Johns, there is probably little that can be compared with one's guilt feeling. But there *is* something worse: the realization that everything is being destroyed without you or anyone else having any part in it."

"The tendency today is away from the accusation," said Dr. Johns. "It will become even more so. The whole tendency in psychiatry is to make man's propensity for sin less and less his own responsibility."

They had taken off their jackets, for it was getting hot on the platform. Only the irregular breathing of the Detective-Sergeant broke the silence that had settled on their ruminations.

"And perhaps we now enter the terrain of the tragic," said Dr. Johns. "Man is inclined to give free rein to his indignation and his sorrow only when there is blame that can be apportioned. When there is no blame, he submits . . ."

"Or he hates, as I do," said Henry.

They looked at the face on the floor of the platform and the face laughed at them. The blue eyes looked from one to the other, but especially at Henry.

"No," said Dr. Johns. "Sorrow and hate are pertinent only if there is blame. And therefore people always seek a scapegoat. Without a scapegoat, mankind cannot bring justice to his hate and sorrow. And . . ." He put on his jacket again as a breeze began to cool his sweaty body. "And the less we are in the position to blame, the greater our need for a scapegoat."

"I do not agree," said Henry.

"It is not hate or grief that you feel," said Dr. Johns. "It's something much deeper, more horrible, something that oppresses you deep within yourself and fills you with fear. Something that" — and he smiled at Henry — "that brings you to seek your refuge in a place like the Foundation."

Detective-Sergeant Demosthenes H. de Goede had finished his exercises and was wiping the sweat from his face and straightening the shoulders of his jacket. He had listened all the time to the conversation and, according to a Pelmanistic method, stored every thought in his memory.

"But it is a ghost that you cannot exorcise," said Dr. Johns. "Therefore, to save yourself, even if you do not wish to know it, you look for a scapegoat." He looked at the moving face of the Giant and the pathetic, never-ceasing smile. "Therefore the tragic figure of our time is perhaps he who takes guilt upon himself to make valid for ourselves our hate or sorrow."

Henry removed his dark glasses. But he replaced them immediately, as if by so doing he could conceal the signs of his vulnerability.

Dr. Johns asked Henry why he dedicated himself with so much enthusiasm to the Foundation. Detective-Sergeant Demosthenes H. de Goede noted, Pelmanistically, Henry's answer that within the bounds of his talents (Dr. Johns surprised at the word "bounds") he did everything in his power to maintain order at Welgevonden, to fulfill order. If this did not come about, as now with the death of Lila, he bore no guilt. Disintegration under the parody of order, had already been there. He could only say that he had done his best. (That merely accentuated the tragedy of the disintegration — Dr. Johns.) There was accordingly nothing else for him to do but to protect the order with renewed energy and dedication against further decay from within, by making the order as secure as possible externally. (But even if he, Henry, were blameless, and even if he lived according to the values of order and fought for the maintenance of order, if the rules of order were today a kind of mockery, if one found that values, sanctified by the years, were today becoming anachronistic, actually unpractical — what then?) Then you were still fighting to preserve everything — for the sake of eternal values. (And if those eternal values, tested in practice, were no longer so eternal and practical, was that morality any longer of any value?) No, he had to acknowledge: then you would have to renounce your values. (And then?) Then there was nothing left for you because you were formed by those values. (Unless?) Unless, of course, the fault lay not with the values, and the disintegration happened as a result of a culpability that could be attributed to someone and . . .

". . . We can find a scapegoat," said Dr. Johns.

"And can prove that the primordial powers of chaos have taken over in the name of order," said Henry.

Detective-Sergeant Demosthenes H. de Goede had now joined them and was threatening to take part in the conversation.

Dr. Johns hastily proposed that they resume their stroll, since time was limited.

In the meantime, the Giant's head had disappeared and Henry declared that he preferred to remain on the platform and meditate further.

"My father-in-law, Jock Silberstein, and I often had conversations here," he said.

They said good-bye and Detective-Sergeant Demosthenes H. de Goede stuttered to Dr. Johns, as they slowly descended the ladder, his admiration for their host, Henry Silberstein-van Eeden.

"You should have known him eighteen years ago, when he had just come here," said Dr. Johns. "He impressed us all with his erudition and his willingness to take part in controversy. These days he is quieter and works harder."

Detective-Sergeant Demosthenes H. de Goede stuttered his last observation before they reached the ground.

"Precisely," said Dr. Johns. "He is very kind to his son. Only a parent could tolerate everything so patiently."

QUIS? · Chapter Ten · The African Quarter, Mon Repos ·· Dr. Johns
decided to take Detective-Sergeant Demosthenes H. de Goede by a roundabout way to the
African quarter before showing him the factory, cellars
and bottling plant. This necessitated their leaving the road
and walking through fields and veld.

"Watch out for snakes," said Dr. Johns. "There may still
be a few here, although Henry Silberstein-van Eeden is trying
systematically to extirpate them."

They walked carefully through the long grass and looked
attentively ahead of them.

"Mind!" screamed Dr. Johns.

Detective-Sergeant Demosthenes H. de Goede leaped athletically into the air, and nimbly seized a stone as he landed on
the ground again. Dr. Johns was kneeling and studying something attentively in the trodden grass. He held up a small
plant.

"How rare! A real *ephialtion*."

He nursed the plant in his hand as they proceeded.

"I sometimes wonder," he said, "if Henry and Salome actually found one another." He took Detective-Sergeant Demosthenes H. de Goede by the arm. "Now that we know
one another better, I might as well tell you of my doubts."

Detective-Sergeant Demosthenes H. de Goede looked
happy.

"Imagine," said Dr. Johns, "that Henry found after a time
that Salome no longer loved him. While he could reproach,
while he could blame himself, for instance, because he could

not satisfy her in some respects, there was always hope. But if he suddenly realized that she no longer loved him and that there was no guilt on his part — he was left with a qualitative judgment of the situation, and so the situation became a thousand times more intolerable. Does that not, perhaps, explain his dedication to the Foundation?" He looked closely at Detective-Sergeant Demosthenes H. de Goede. "If, one fine day, one finds incontrovertible evidence that something is vanishing and being reduced to nothing, what does one do then?" When Detective-Sergeant Demosthenes H. de Goede answered with difficulty, Dr. Johns laughed. "I see you have paid close attention. You are quite right: you do your best, you would move the earth to prevent the break up, to prove to yourself that you can win back lost love. You would, like Henry, devote the whole of your life to something like the Foundation, in which you see the harmony that you associate with her. And if that harmony, too, is threatened and reminds you of her love which, inexplicably, has gone to ruin in a similar way, what are you to do then?"

Detective-Sergeant Demosthenes H. de Goede had his answer ready.

"Exactly," said Dr. Johns. "Then you, like all of us, would be obliged to accept a scapegoat for the sake of your soul's peace."

He walked on pensively.

"I do not envy you your task," said Dr. Johns, "but I envy Henry still less his torment of soul when he presently discovers, on that platform, that he must admit the existence of the scapegoat."

Detective-Sergeant Demosthenes H. de Goede's attention
had wandered, because he had just seen something. In the middle of the field in which they were walking was an immense
bronze statue of a gigantic animal. It gleamed in the sun like
the observation tower and dominated the entire landscape.

"That's a statue of Brutus the bull," said Dr. Johns, "erected
by the Ollenwaar Stud Breeders' Association." He pointed
out words engraved in gold on a certain part of its anatomy.
"Ollenwaar tribute and Ollenwaar gratitude. Erected by the
Red-Black Stud Breeders' Association."

As they stood looking in admiration at the statue, they were
unaware of a man who was lying on his back looking up into
the sky in the shadow of the huge replica. It was the well-beloved Dries van Schalkwyk and he had just had a vision. He
had, as was his habit when in doubt (and had he not begun to
doubt when, a few moments before, he wondered if Brutus
III was perchance not too small) taken refuge at the statue of
Brutus — to admire Brutus' faults, to despise his brute
strength, to belittle his dynamic spirit, to adjure the erotic
nightmare by confrontation in the clear light of day. He had,
in the past, always returned with renewed faith in his breeding policy and with the feeling that Uncle Giepie, in his prophetic vision, would understand. But today he found no help.
There was even a moment when the feared Brutus aroused
a forbidden longing in him. He was about to return to his
room when he saw the vision. Dries van Schalkwyk, secretary
of the R.B.S.B.A., had seen before his eyes the spirit of Uncle
Giepie float, arms outstretched in blessing, over Welgevonden.

Suddenly he heard a voice and leaped up — after the vision

ready for the annunciation — and then he saw Dr. Johns and Detective-Sergeant Demosthenes H. de Goede. He gave them a friendly greeting but told them nothing of his visitation. That was a revelation for himself alone. He hurried off and met the Giant who had been following Dr. Johns and Detective-Sergeant Demosthenes H. de Goede. Once again fury rose in him, but this time without that feeling of powerlessness. The sign was there! Retribution would follow! The moment was full of meaning!

"This is the African quarter, Mon Repos," said Dr. Johns as they drew nearer the symmetrical network of houses. "It, too, is part of the Foundation."

In the middle of a clump of trees, which were all dying simultaneously because their bark had been stripped off, was an arch, over the gate that gave admittance to the quarter, with the single word "Welcome" painted on it. Next to the gate were a number of notices warning all visitors in choice English not to do certain things like spitting, committing acts of vandalism or loafing around. Directly before the gate a Blantyre, against a background of his own handiwork, was surrounded by an admiring crowd of intellectual visitors, eminent guests and several proud residents and relatives. A shining black guide and his white colleague were pointing out, describing and explaining every object.

Madam Ritchie, when she saw Dr. Johns and Detective-Sergeant Demosthenes H. de Goede join the group, greeted the reunion exuberantly. Hope and Prudence, their hair in soft locks over their shoulders, looked shyly at Detective-Ser-

geant Demosthenes H. de Goede and lowered their eyes modestly. There was a blush on their cheeks and Detective-Sergeant Demosthenes H. de Goede stuttered a rapid question in
Dr. Johns' ear.

"It's difficult to say," said Dr. Johns as they followed the
guides through the gate. "I know that one is a resident and
the other, of course, a relative — but I can't say offhand
which." He reflected for a moment. "Perhaps Prudence . . .
no, Hope . . ." He shook his head. "I am sorry, but it's so
difficult to remember."

The guides drew attention to the walls of the entrance, on
which numerous photographs of laughing Africans were dis-
played. Each African had been photographed with his arms
full of rand notes, and below something was written in
three languages: Xosa, Sotho and Venda.

The black guide translated: "Bonamie Shekudu receives his
award for services beyond the call of duty. Bonamie raised
the alarm at the time of the beer hall fire. Bonamie distinguished himself at the extinguishment of the flames."

"Benjamin M'Kodo refused to burn his identity card . . ."

"Nukunu Bubu planted three hundred and thirty-three
trees . . ."

One of the intellectual visitors spotted other photographs
hidden away behind screens and he approached one of the
guides. White guide and black conferred together and then
the black guide said that they had decided, perhaps contrary
to regulations, to show the rest of the photographs, since it
was a special occasion (indicating the eminent guests). Ladies
were requested not to look. Madam Ritchie was the first to

shriek as the screens were removed to show a series of photographs of Africans hanging rigid from sneezewood gallows.

"Shemane Babete, B.A., LL.B., paid the ultimate penalty for taking part in the rites of manducation."

"Shikudu M'pane paid the ultimate penalty for decapitating his mother and using her eyes for *muti*."

Both guides explained that the photographs served as deterrents.

An intellectual visitor asked the white guide to pose next to one of the photographs. A close-up was taken of only the faces without captions, for overseas distribution. Several of the visitors competed to be taken: as also Madam Ritchie, with many gestures and much chattering. She was rapidly becoming a "personality" and had already exchanged addresses with one of the eminent visitors.

The Giant had also joined the group and was unexpectedly taken by one of the photographers, as he was grinning broadly, next to one of the gallows scenes.

After that they were all taken to the reception office to be shown the layout of the township on maps. The room filled from wall to wall and the guides had to stand on tables as they explained that there was a quartz mine under the terrain and that one of the big companies was mining it in conjunction with the Foundation. A photograph of the chairman of the directorate was pointed out: the open, unprejudiced, sensitive face of a great liberal, known for his progressive tendencies and political influence behind the scenes. Although he would have liked to remain anonymous, everyone recognized him at once as Julius Johnson.

Outside, the white guide was explaining a system of identi-
fication by which each African inhabitant or relative was
known by a band around his head.

"The color of the band," said the white guide, "indicates the
individual's period of service in the mine and residence as an
inhabitant of the township. It's quite simple: white, blue,
green, yellow and red, respectively, for one to five years,
with scarlet for ten years, after which the inhabitant concerned is discharged, with the right to stay on for a second
decade as relative-inhabitant or relative-worker, with similar
color distinctions, namely, half-white, half-blue, half-green,
half-yellow, half-red to half-scarlet for the following service
period of ten years."

At this point several visitors asked questions.

Detective-Sergeant Demosthenes H. de Goede, instructed
long ago, naturally, at the police college regarding the system,
confined his attention to the shy Misses Hope and Prudence,
who understood nothing and repeatedly asked him to explain,
as they looked blindingly into his eyes.

The group was then taken to the community center.

"The sports fields," said the black guide and pointed to a
group of black inhabitants kicking a soccer ball back and forth
in clouds of dust (despite recent rains). They juggled cleverly
with the ball, bouncing it from knee, shoulder, head, heel and
side of foot, tapping it to and fro, shooting it between their
own legs and stopping it with the tip of the boot. On the
sidelines were a number of black inhabitants stretched out on
benches and following the game with expressionless faces and
who, at the appearance of the guides and their group, im-

mediately directed their attention as expressionlessly at the new manifestation.

The game was stopped at a sign from the black guide, who occupied an important position in the hierarchy of the model township. The two captains, wearing blue and red bands respectively, were introduced to a few eminent visitors and photographed. Then one of the well-known guests was talked into kicking off, after Madam Ritchie had with great difficulty been balked in her intention of doing so herself. The eminent American guest kicked the heavy ball slap into the dust clouds, while everyone crowded around and slapped him heartily on the back.

The two guides smiled broadly at the singular success of their important visit. Things could so easily go wrong. There was, for instance, the murder two nights ago of the white girl Lila, which might have ruined everything — but all was going briskly and well.

In a moment of improvisation, the white guide invited Detective-Sergeant Demosthenes H. de Goede to take part in the game for a few minutes. He did so without hesitation. He bounced in among the black inhabitants, juggled the ball with them, bumped them away like rag dolls with his muscular shoulders and made a dead set for the goal. At the last moment, with the net open to him, he passed the ball to one of the black players who, applauding himself thunderously, bounced it from foot to knee, and from knee to head, into the net. It was a masterly handling of the situation by the Detective-Sergeant who consummated the bonhomie fittingly.

On the way to the medical quarters, with the two appealing girls, Hope and Prudence, linked to each of his arms, Detec-

tive-Sergeant Demosthenes H. de Goede as well as the rest of
the party was unaware of the Giant who had appeared on the
field and launched an attack on the ball. The players left the
field and gathered with the spectators, grumbling, under a tree,
from where they all watched the Giant with hostile faces.
Alone on the field, with the ball at his feet, he looked smilingly
at the group under the tree and then at the goal. Suddenly he
kicked. The ball glanced off the side of his shoe, rolled over
the ground, over the boundary, away in the midday sun.

"The pharmacy, hospital with fourteen beds and quarters of
of the doctor," said the white guide and introduced the female
mission doctor to them; against a background of colored bottles along the wall, she at once called upon them for funds.
She revealed certain statistics to them and mentioned a new
wing that had to be built. She led them through rooms tiled
from side to side in white. "Easy to wash," she explained. She
showed them her patients in the reception hall who, with colored bands around their heads, looked vaguely sick. She led
them to an adjoining room where a single bed in pure white
isolation stood exactly in the middle of a shining floor. "This
is where we handle emergency cases," said she, the mission
doctor, and conjured up visions for them. (From blood-warm
Africa certain basic facts about life.) Her silent wish was made
a reality when a black inhabitant with a split skull was at that
very moment brought in; this gave her the opportunity to be
photographed, for an international magazine, with her finger
in the wound. She took leave of the guests to pose for more
photos: exhausted beside a paraffin lamp, washing herself in an

earthenware bowl on a soapbox — the bags under her eyes attributable to dedication, not dissipation.

She was about fifty years of age and not unattractive. Her skin was dull, her eyes soft and her figure masculine. Her predecessor had been devoured by Shemane Babete, B.A., LL.B. She had a secret wish that was indescribable. She ameliorated suffering and campaigned for a healthy body and universal suffrage. The cameras clicked continuously and the eminent visitors declared themselves proud to be photographed with her.

Both guides found it imperative to draw the attention of the group to passing time: it was already late, and a great deal lay ahead.

There followed fleeting impressions of a kitchen with cast-iron pots over fires and the sour smell of mealie porridge being warmed up. There were impressions of a recreation hall with a Ping-Pong table in the middle, darts on the walls, CNA periodicals on stands, photos of black women on the walls. Everywhere there were black inhabitants taking part in no game, who looked at no photo of black women and did not say a word.

One of the intellectual woman guests started a conversation. She asked a big black inhabitant in pidgin English where he came from and if he were married. He said something in his own language and a group around him burst out laughing. She saw that he wore a red band and asked him (proud of her knowledge) if he already had been with the Foundation for five years. He took no notice of her and she smiled at him. That was no good, so she asked him if he had children, pickaninnies. He simply looked at her. She told him that she was a visitor from Sweden, and that did not help, either. She offered him a cigarette and he put it behind his ear. She was still trying to establish contact with him when the guests left the hall and her friend plucked at her arm.

The Giant had come into the hall sometime after the others and walked right across the middle of it. The darts on the walls attracted his attention and he pocketed two of them. The black inhabitants at the door contemplated barring his way, but slowly gave way as the big figure loomed up.

A quick visit to the butchery (white tiles, meat in refrigerated rooms): "They eat the same food as we do" (the white guide).

There was a longer pause at the Native shop, especially to give the eminent overseas guests an opportunity to make purchases. The colored Bantu blankets, manufactured by a factory in Ladybrand, were first on the list. Hand-threaded bead objects second. (Especially the kind to which a story, supplied by the black guide, was attached: "If she hasn't had a man yet; she's looking for a man. . . .") Detective-Sergeant Demosthenes H. de Goede bought one of each of these for Hope and Prudence, to the great delight of everybody. Madam Ritchie pretended to be angry, and the black inhabitant-customers watched with expressionless faces.

Crossing the dusty square, loaded with purchases, the expedition began to tell on the visitors. The dust blew in their eyes, the trees in their dying hour gave scant shade. At a huge white screen ("Outdoor theater," said the black guide) they found a large crowd of black inhabitants. They walked past somewhat faster when the black guide began talking to one of the black inhabitants. He shot out his sentences like machine-gun bullets and ended the conversation with a rapid fusillade of words and raised his shoulders. After that he was noticeably quieter.

"There's something in the air," said Dr. Johns to Detective-Sergeant Demosthenes H. de Goede, who narrowed his eyes and sniffed the air. He moved his shoulders and thrust out his chin. He stuttered something to Dr. Johns and looked here and there around him, as if scanning the whole area for exits, hiding places and entrenchments.

A shrill whistle sounded in the distance and then the ululation of women's voices. The crowd stirred and then everything was quiet again.

The guests now walked decidedly faster and closer together across the square to where a cafeteria sign welcomed them. They seemed visibly to relax when they saw the Coca-Cola advertisements and the chromium soda fountain inside. A laughing black inhabitant behind the counter quickly restored their spirits by asking cheerfully what they would like.

"With the compliments of the Foundation," said the black guide, looking abstractedly through the door at the black crowd in the distance.

The guests had recovered exuberantly: the women guests threw the Bantu blankets over their shoulders and paraded before the men; the men did all sorts of amusing things with the beads. The guides had some difficulty in moving the guests on to the next phase of the tour: the men had taken off their jackets and loosened their ties; the women had pow-

dered their noses and found the toilet arrangements a problem
— except the woman from Sweden, who went and returned
without a scratch, to hold herself, in liberal self-sufficiency,
aloof from the rest of the guests for the remainder of the expedition.

The next place was reassuringly near one of the big exit
gates and they entered a room full of black inhabitants im-
mersed in newspapers, encyclopedias and historical works.

"The library," said the black guide, to the great excitement of the intellectual visitors. The woman from Sweden, in
particular, was ecstatic when she leaned over shoulders and
recognized the cover of a book by her beloved Bertrand
Russell in the hands of one of the black inhabitants. She found
a twin soul in laughing white teeth and black eyes which,
more effectively even than aloofness, succeeded in setting her
apart. The eminent visitors looked through the bookshelves
and asked for more photographs. There was temporary dis-
organization when the black inhabitants were invited to join
the groups to be photographed. Everyone had a jolly time
there and left the library very happy, waving and allowing
the inhabitants to return to their chairs and try to find the
exact places in their books again.

On their way to the next room they were confronted by a
couple of black tots who shoved a pamphlet into the hand of
each of them. A little farther on they came across a row of
children with white sashes across their bodies, placards held
in front of their chests and black eyes fixed motionless on the
center of the square. The guides held aloof and lit cigarettes
while the visitors read the pamphlets and placards.

"FREE JULIUS JOOL!"
"JULIUS JOOL MUST GO FREE!"
"FREEDOM FOR JULIUS JOOL!"

The eminent visitors wanted to know who Julius Jool was, but got no information from the children, who commanded no English or advanced ideas. The guides refrained from any comment. It was left to Dr. Johns to explain and, of course, he began with that aspect of Julius Jool's nature which was of interest to him.

"Julius Jool is a hermaphrodite and a firebug," Dr. Johns told the visitors. He expatiated on the universal melody of masculine and feminine tonality, the product of Aphrodite and Hermes, the prehuman undifferentiated condition. He mentioned the bisexual creature born from an egg. He spoke of the Ganymede on a dolphin. He took them back to the birth of the primordial child from water and related it to the birth of Aphrodite, according to Hesiod.

As he spoke, the black children suddenly began to chant: "FREE JULIUS JOOL!" "FREE JULIUS JOOL!"

He referred to the birth of the doomed Titans from the intercourse of Heaven and Earth, Gaea and Uranus. He told about Cronus who emasculated his father with his left hand and flung the phallus in the sea. He looked in particular at Detective-Sergeant Demosthenes H. de Goede and told of the birth of Aphrodite from the foam — the end and beginning of ontogenesis, the incomprehensible conjunction of the phallus that became a child, the reconciliation of opposites. He referred also to the birth of the mythological Giants, and Detective-Sergeant Demosthenes H. de Goede nodded understandingly; and to the children of the phallus, the primitive phenomena born of the emasculation, blood brothers of the erotic spirit and the tormenting Erinyes.

He struggled to convey to the fascinated guests and eminent visitors an incomprehensible idea, while the black children, with staring eyes, renewed their refrain: "JULIUS JOOL FOR FREEDOM! JULIUS JOOL FOR FREEDOM!"

At this stage, before he could expatiate on the incendiary inclinations of the hermaphroditic martyr, the guides intervened and drew attention again to the limited time available to the honored guests. After a photograph had been taken of the Swedish woman with a child in her arms, the group moved on.

They came now to the last room, where a resident occupational guidance officer saw to it that every black inhabitant took a regular efficiency test. He explained one such test, which required the candidate to construct a cubic whole from asymmetrical blocks. Several of the guests were invited to have a try, but they all proved unwilling, except Madam Ritchie, who made a hopeless botch of the whole thing and, laughing cheerfully, fell back on feminine helplessness to save her face. One of the eminent visitors was pushed forward by a colleague, and he made a joke of the whole affair. After his first attempt one block remained. The whole process was repeated while everyone watched with interest and the eminent guest rapidly lost his temper as he realized that this time another spare block would remain over.

"The black inhabitants succeed about seventy percent of the time," said the black guide contentedly. "Those who are not successful are confined to small jobs that don't require much competence or responsibility."

The eminent visitor declared, when he was halfway through his third attempt, that he did not have time to complete it, but he described in the minutest detail by what principles it should be completed. He stepped back and looked longingly outside. Then he was saved by the entry of the Giant, who picked up the blocks and looked at them, while the guests nodded at each other and waited to see what would happen. The Giant's clumsy hands covered the blocks, shook them, fumbled with them and suddenly put down a completed cubic unit on the table. Everyone left the room while the Giant, captivated by the new toy, completed the cubic unit again and again in various ways.

Outside, they found the square filled with black inhabitants moving about restlessly. Every now and then they looked up into the sky and then, with clearly apparent hostility, at the guests. The two guides increased their pace and tried to take a circular course around the crowd, and the guests, encumbered by their heavy purchases, tried to keep up with them. They were quickly encircled by a stream of black inhabitants who had come from another quarter.

The black guide spoke again to one of the visitors and Hope and Prudence clung to Detective-Sergeant Demosthenes H. de Goede's arms. He drew the two girls more closely to him and looked around with calculation. One of the eminent visitors asked the white guide what was happening, and the guide repeated the question to the black guide in an African language.

"A short while ago they saw a human being floating through the air," said the white guide. "It was the spirit of their ancestors, with its arms spread out over the township."

The white guide was undecided whether he should proceed and the eminent visitor took him aside.

"It's a sign," whispered the white guide, "that their ancestors are calling upon them to take over the land over which his spirit has floated. They must destroy everything his shadow fell upon and purify the land. They must destroy the evil spirits and purify the land with fire and blood."

The leading phalanx of black inhabitants began stamping the ground rhythmically with their feet. The monotonous rhythm urged them on to more energetic movements and all of a sudden one of them leaped into the air with a blood-curdling cry. The ululation of women came from a distance and a shrill whistle tore the air.

The eminent guest who had had difficulty with the cubic unit regained considerable respect by helping the two guides with the removal of the women guests through the crowd, which gave way willingly. They had some difficulty with the woman from Sweden, who insisted on staying behind and taking part in the mass demonstration. They ignored the Giant, however, who joined the mob. He had begun to dance with those in the vanguard, his thundering feet sounding louder than theirs, his appearance more threatening, his abandon equal to theirs. He was blissfully unaware of the glowering eyes watching him with twofold hatred, with their primordial fear of the monster, of the aberrant mind that communicated with evil spirits, and with their hatred of the color of his skin, upon which all their grievances were projected.

When everyone had passed through the gates, and were reminded of their recent adventure only by the shrill whistling and the ululation, they all sighed with wonderful relief. It had been an instructive visit. They were all full of praise for the Foundation and the officials. The guides were freely given tips and, in their turn, each visitor received a piece of colored ribbon. (The Giant arrived in time to get a scarlet ribbon.)

At the gate everyone bought some of the Blantyre's wares: brightly polished *panga* blades of various designs. The guides had, however, a last request — just outside the township, on a hillock above a small lily-covered lake fed by water from the masks, an interdenominational church for the black inhabitants had been built in typical style. It was safe there and worth a visit.

The guests, now guideless, followed a footpath paved with stone and reached the lake below the little church. They admired the lilies and the fish and then climbed the hillock to the church. Going around a corner, Madam Ritchie suddenly let out a stifled shriek and the guests ran forward. They saw a man with a long beard who had come out of the bushes beside Madam Ritchie. He was without shoes and shirt. They stared at him in astonishment but he maintained his dignity, in spite of his appearance. He explained that he was Reverend Williams, that he had bathed in the lake and on his return had found that someone had stolen his shirt. He hoped that everyone, considering the unusual circumstances, would excuse him. He looked at the church on the hill: the construction with the colored windows and the roof like that on a huge rondavel, and he offered to explain to the visitors some interesting aspects of the building. He had often preached there in the past.

With Reverend Williams, shirtless, in the lead, they approached, ascending, the gigantic rondavel church on the hill. They were, however, just too late to see the interior, for as they reached the summit of the hill, the first flames leaped from the roof and smoke billowed up into the blue sky.

The conflagration, however, was something to see. It would have satisfied the deepest urges of Julius Jool, absent, under house arrest. It was a conflagration which at that moment seemed to fill the heavens and offered many opportunities for the most beautiful color photographs.

·· "I only hope that there is no repetition of eighteen years ago," said Dr. Johns as he looked back at the smoke column that hung over the hillock like a volcanic cloud. "We have put up a good many new buildings, but living room is severely limited."

They were now descending slightly and walking through a valley where arum lilies grew beside streams. Then they ascended a slight rise and could see the masks on the slopes.

"The trout lake is there, just around the bend," said Dr. Johns and pointed. On the crest of the hill the factory, cellars and bottling plant gleamed in the distance. In the meantime they wandered through wet heather and past pools of water.

They came across a herd of skinny heifers.

"They're not Welgevonden animals," said Dr. Johns. "*They* were bought for experimental purposes."

A little farther on they came across Brutus III, the bull, on his back, his legs erect as poles in the air. Dr. Johns gave him a light kick behind the shoulder and the little bull struggled up, lowing with pain. He trotted a short distance with them and then spotted another group of heifers in the distance. He rushed through the heather, his voice raised to an awful bellow that dwindled into a plaintive cry of fear when, as so often before, he collapsed in the heather among them and died his particular temporary death.

"It is said," remarked Dr. Johns to Detective-Sergeant

Demosthenes H. de Goede, "that our well-beloved field worker got his inspiration for his fertilization formula from the cultivators of the bastard mealie seed, P.P.K. 64. The male is also a weak, sere, pathetic plant."

They had now reached an entrance hall that led into the cellars. Beside it was a small office in which an ancient, toothless resident wrote his name in a stylish, shaky hand on an admission form and handed it to them.

"Remember the function tomorrow night," he said, mumbling his piece. "A full attendance will be appreciated."

They passed through dripping tunnels which imperceptibly descended to cellars. The walls were overgrown with moss and the sound of their footsteps rang dully against them. Everywhere in the vaults that followed were empty vats in which, once, wines had matured. The entire place was a museum in which was exhibited the complete process of grape juice — through fermentation — to wine. Names were neatly printed on placards; the history was indicated, step by step and from room to room, on labels; all the containers and the complete framework were there — only the contents were lacking. It was like one of those anthropological museums in which display cases contain skulls, artifacts and implements that span the centuries, and only life is absent.

In one of the vaults they came across Jock Silberstein. He was sitting in a chair beside a wooden table on which there were all sorts of goblets and pipettes that, in the old days, had been used by the wine tasters to determine the quality of the wine. His hands were clasped behind his head and he was peacefully snoozing, like someone who had a wearying day behind him. He was somewhat confused when he woke up and saw them.

"Have you by any chance seen Adam Kadmon?" he said immediately.

"He was with us a while ago," said Dr. Johns.

"What did he look like?" asked Jock Silberstein. "I mean, there was nothing the matter with him?"

"There was nothing the matter," said Dr. Johns.

"They hate him," said Jock Silberstein. "I can feel it in the air." Suddenly he heard something, listened attentively and then relaxed. "There is something inviolate about him; something that embraces all nature, which has nothing to do with reason, that represents the natural forces. If only they would realize this." The sounds now reached them more clearly and became identifiable as heavy footsteps. "If they would only see him as a child, helpless and powerless in their world, but filled with all the primordial power of instinct and the untamableness of nature."

At that moment the Giant arrived and seemed, although apparently innocent, monstrous in the cellar. Jock Silberstein jumped up hurriedly from the chair and went to meet him. The caressing words he spoke were inappropriate, the fondling of the clumsy creature banal, the childish gestures with which the fondling was rejected, grotesque.

"They hate him," Jock grumbled fondly, "they hate him, my poor child . . ."

Dr. Johns and Detective-Sergeant Demosthenes H. de Goede left the cellar, embarrassed. They looked back and saw the Giant still brushing off the caresses.

Outside, Dr. Johns took Detective-Sergeant Demosthenes H. de Goede to a small room next to the factory. Inside it, against the walls, were numerous copper pipes that intertwined and were connected to a steam boiler outside.

"It is an interesting place," said Dr. Johns. "Henry Silberstein-van Eeden once told me that Jock Silberstein, when he was still actively engaged in farming, called it his room of confession."

The Detective-Sergeant stuttered a question.

"At that time, I never really understood," said Dr. Johns and peered inquisitively around the room. "I fancy he told me that Jock Silberstein opened the steam cock and then experienced a sort of spiritual release from what followed." He indicated the various instruments. "Shall we try?" He suddenly opened one of the taps and a deafening noise filled the room. They remained speechless, listening to the monotonous noise and said and stuttered something to one another that was inaudible. Only their mouths opened and shut. Dr. Johns closed the tap and said: "Extraordinary. Simply a noise." He looked around the room again. "Perhaps Henry did not tell the full story. Perhaps there is something else." He opened the tap again, and then another; in the noise the room suddenly filled with steam so that they both gradually disappeared from one another in the mist.

At one moment they were still able to see one another, their mouths open to shout inaudible instructions to one another, the next they were frighteningly alone in an invisible world that made them feel more alone than people who had got lost in the mist on a mountain slope. The ceaseless noise

grew louder, the mist glowed white as if it were itself a source
of light. The noise came from all sides, their eyes were wide
open in their attempt to see something through the moving
white. There was a demoniac roaring in that ghastly solitude:
a different hell from what one had imagined; it was unfamiliar
to one's conception of darkness and the known images of fear.
This was something indescribably new: a Hades without
monsters, a bleak Hades without content, a Hades that kept
one captive in a continuum of meaningless sound. It was not a
room of confession and spiritual release, but a room of super-
natural torment, and Detective-Sergeant Demosthenes H.
de Goede felt himself flinging cry after cry of terror into
nothingness.

And then, suddenly, he felt his tongue free; that pure,
clear words which he could not hear were describing his solitude and fear. Detective-Sergeant Demosthenes H. de Goede
— at the precise moment when he felt fear as he had never
felt it at the police college and in his dangerous career, when
he was fighting in this underworld against an enemy that he
had never encountered before — rid himself temporarily of
that defect which had burdened him throughout his life. His
silver tongue articulated his fear in the most beautiful language; he was endowed suddenly with a power that had always been denied him: to give lucid expression to his deepest
feelings. At that moment of unendurable suffering he experienced also his deepest wish fulfillment and greatest triumph. There was even a time when, in his cries of anguish,
he welcomed suffering for the sake of his new freedom of
speech. But it did not last long. Slowly but surely his fear
grew greater and he became accustomed to that desired free-

dom. He was in the act of selling his soul to the evil spirits and he stumbled wildly around the room to destroy the contact. Screaming, groping and terrified, he fell and beat against the wall and the pipes until he reached the cocks and, with a last effort of strength, turned them off.

The mist cleared gradually and the noise stopped at once. And gradually the two figures in the room became visible. Dr. Johns, small and shrunken, in a corner: an old man, wet with sweat, and with the aftermath of indescribable fear in his eyes; and Detective-Sergeant Demosthenes H. de Goede: sweat shining on his face, the powerful muscles of his arms swollen to bursting, his face lifted as he ejaculated a flood of mangled words that gradually subsided to a pathetic stutter.

In the silence that followed he tried to say something to Dr. Johns, but when he failed to do so, he kept resignedly quiet and wiped the mist from his eyes.

They walked slowly away and did not see the Giant who had watched their every movement. The huge figure was about to enter the room when Jock Silberstein appeared, took him gently by the hand and led him away against his will.

They reached the hall known as the bottling plant, but had difficulty in getting in because of the crush caused by two streams of visitors who had arrived at the same time.

"I can't help it," said one guide to the other, "the well-beloved Dries' speech was cut short by an hour."

Dr. Johns showed Detective-Sergeant Demosthenes H. de Goede through a window a row of bottles that came sailing past on a conveyer belt, were filled and vanished through a monastic tunnel next door.

"Glutamic acid and thiamine," said Dr. Johns.

In the hall next door, labels were put on the bottles by an intricate machine. Against the wall was a huge accounting machine. Various residents were performing all sorts of tasks, clothed in the Welgevonden uniforms. Dr. Johns had considerable difficulty in getting Detective-Sergeant Demosthenes H. de Goede away from the crowds.

"You've probably already wondered," Dr. Johns said to Detective-Sergeant Demosthenes H. de Goede, who looked back longingly at the crowds as they walked on, "what Henry and I mean by order and chaos?" He repeated the question until he had his companion's full attention. "I have often reflected on it and come to the following conclusion: it is the organized world of reason against the powers of the unconscious, the differentiated world of the civilized man against the undifferentiated primordial world from which he developed by the momentum of his will."

He found it even more difficult to hold Detective-Sergeant Demosthenes H. de Goede's attention when they passed through a garden where red and yellow flowers were in the process of becoming bastardized and filling the courtyard of a square building with garish particolor.

"The development of reasoning was a great development," said Dr. Johns. "Man acquired a soul and he must fight with all the powers at his disposal to protect that soul against the monster in his dark past."

They were overwhelmed by the blaze of colors on their way to a small building at the side of the factory.

"It is the task of the hero to triumph over darkness," said Dr. Johns. "The triumph of the rational over the great and dangerous unconscious. Society wishes to project its struggle in the struggle of its champion."

He found it necessary first to stop Detective-Sergeant Demosthenes H. de Goede before they entered the room, where a small group was assembled.

"Society is helpless without its champion," said Dr. Johns. "The more it itself employs its own will toward order, the more it is removed from the soil in which it roots; its freedom of will becomes a source of transgression against its deep-rooted instincts. In its dilemma it needs a crucifixion, someone to die in the name of chaos, a sacrifice of atonement to protect it against the primitive powers that threaten to falsify its order."

Dr. Johns observed that Detective-Sergeant Demosthenes H. de Goede was not listening and he was about to throw in the sponge when he saw the Giant walking through the flowers hand in hand with Jock.

"The Giant-child is the legendary personification of the powers of chaos," he said slyly. "It's a primordial child who in his inviolability embraces all nature." He nodded encouragingly as Detective-Sergeant Demosthenes H. de Goede began now to take an interest. Something he had learned at the police college was dawning. "It's a powerful being," said Dr. Johns, "with the vulnerability of a child. It commands all the powers of free nature: primitive and unrestrained."

He was satisfied when Detective-Sergeant Demosthenes H. de Goede narrowed his eyes to slits, began rolling his shoulders and disappeared purposefully through the crowd into the room.

*

The speaker, introduced by the guide, was Professor Dreyer
— a man with wavy white hair, sunk motionless in thought
on the platform by the window, his students leaning in rows
against the wall on either side of him, their bored attention
fixed on the visitors as they prepared to listen to him. The
wall was covered with shelves full of test tubes and glass containers in which various colored liquids shone in the sun. Professor Dreyer waited until the room was quite silent, so that
only the noise of the masks in the distance could be heard,
and then he began his talk.

He welcomed everyone on behalf of himself and his students. He disposed of his annual joke, while the students
looked at each other, and then began with an explanation of
his work. He would put it as simply and popularly as possible, so that everyone could understand. The eyes of the
guests were soon glazed with concentration, and they left
each other for a spiritual siesta as the voice and the masks
droned on monotonously. The hypnotic text was perpetual
fermentation: the complicated connection was the psychic
implication of zymosis and libido. Schooled by church and
community life, they suffered passively the particular didactic,
as a variation of their thirst for knowledge. Once they were
plucked back from the lassitude of their rumination to inspect
a test tube, in which four layers of four different colored
liquids turned gray when moved and then reverted to motionless separation. Then the audience was allowed to subside
into reverie, to the lullaby of abstruse explanation.

Half an hour passed in which beginning, middle and end
were disposed of, and then they all returned with a shock to
reality when Professor Dreyer, by way of a *coda*, suddenly

changed his theme and began talking about a raped virgin called Lila.

The residents had known her as someone with a heart full of love. Was she not always willing to have a friendly little chat with everyone? A smile here, a little encouragement there. She often visited the laboratory (the students would corroborate) to ask how things were going there. (The students lowered their eyes to their hands.)

A layman, true; but not ashamed of her ignorance.

(There were tears in the old man's eyes.)

He called her friend, and now she was gone.

(During the funeral service he had embalmed her in his heart. He *was* the only one! Indescribable delight, like the ideal fermentation, indefinitely prolonged . . .)

He apologized for losing control of himself and for having had to end off, before the eminent visitors, with a reference to this tragic event. But it lay close to the heart of everybody at Welgevonden, and as he had been informed that the person in charge of the investigation was also in the audience, he wished simply to take advantage of this opportunity to wish him all success in his important task and, on behalf of everyone in the laboratory, to express his regret and, Dr. Johns, to ask you to convey this to those concerned.

Professor Dreyer left the platform in silence, followed by his students. They resumed work (among the test tubes). The visitors recognized Detective-Sergeant Demosthenes H. de Goede and nodded amiably. Then they quietly followed the guide outside and allowed Dr. Johns and the Detective-Sergeant to continue their important perambulation undisturbed.

QUIS? · Chapter Twelve · Dreyer
the Oracle and the Cottage with the
Asbestos Roof ·· There were all the signs
that the day was drawing to an end: the sun lay low
on the horizon, the clouds in the west had already been
touched with the first rose and would later turn to a garish
red, so typical of the country.

"The eminent visitors will enjoy the sunset," said Dr. Johns.
"I am glad that they will have the opportunity to see such a
thing at Welgevonden. Our nature is one of our most valuable
instruments of propaganda."

Dr. Johns walked slightly ahead and led Detective-Sergeant
Demosthenes H. de Goede thus, unnoticed, toward another
row of cottages. The one they were now approaching was
certainly one of the gayest. It was surrounded by hollyhocks
and carnations and there were so many flowers and creepers
that the cottage could hardly be noticed. It looked like a piece
of garden that was inhabited. Dr. Johns opened the red garden
gate and motioned Detective-Sergeant Demosthenes H. de
Goede to enter.

He knocked at the green door and, as they waited, told him
where they were and whom they were to meet.

"It's Mrs. Dreyer, the wife of Professor Dreyer, to whom we
have just listened." He tilted his head to listen to a sound
coming from the cottage. "It is said that eighteen years ago
she was Jock Silberstein's mistress. It is difficult to believe and
is probably one of those malicious rumors so often circulated
about the owner of a place like Welgevonden." The sounds
were now recognizable as footsteps. "Mrs. Dreyer is our

Oracle of Delphi," said Dr. Johns hastily. "She is the best fortune-teller in the whole Republic."

The footsteps had come up to the door and stopped.

Detective-Sergeant Demosthenes H. de Goede took out his handkerchief and wiped his hands.

"No," said Dr. Johns, "she uses teacups. Only Mazawattee tea is drunk, and remember to use your left hand because you are unmarried."

The door opened and a plump little woman well in her fifties, dressed in a light, floral dress, invited them to enter without greeting them. She led them to a small sitting room, asked them to be seated and disappeared toward the kitchen.

Dr. Johns and Detective-Sergeant Demosthenes H. de Goede sat upright in their chairs and listened to the sound of teacups clinking. They could clearly hear Mrs. Dreyer's kettle begin to sing as she did various small domestic chores. Now and then the telephone rang and they listened to Mrs. Dreyer making an appointment for this or that time. The sitting room was well polished and there were desert scenes on the walls and shepherdesses on the sideboard. Old Christmas decorations still hung in a corner and in another corner a model airplane was suspended from a string. The mats on the floor were colorful and had recently been dry-cleaned.

Detective-Sergeant Demosthenes H. de Goede asked Dr. Johns' permission to light a cigarette and looked around the spotless room for a place to dispose of his match. Dr. Johns showed him a glittering ashtray in the form of a gondola on the little table next to his chair. Beside it was a portrait of Jock Silberstein, and also one of the Queen of England.

"Remember it costs fifty cents," said Dr. Johns. "Ten cents for the Foundation and forty for herself."

Detective-Sergeant Demosthenes H. de Goede took out the money in anticipation and put it on the table.

Mrs. Dreyer suddenly appeared in the room and with difficulty took a milk jug from a shelf above a cupboard on which water jugs, glasses and crockery were accurately arranged in a straight row. Her dress stretched to bursting point as she reached up to take the milk jug. Detective-Sergeant Demosthenes H. de Goede was just too late to help her, but she said nothing. She merely pulled her dress down and bowed her head like someone who has withdrawn from the world. Then she left them.

A little later there was a shuffling at the door and Dr. Johns opened it. Mrs. Dreyer brought in a tray with a single cup of tea on it. She offered it to Detective-Sergeant Demosthenes H. de Goede and went out again.

Detective-Sergeant Demosthenes H. de Goede took three spoonfuls of sugar, stirred and drank the cup at a single draft. A whole mouthful of tea leaves remained on his tongue and he spat them carefully back. He had hardly shaken the cup three times with his left hand when Mrs. Dreyer returned suddenly and sat down in front of him on a stool.

She looked attentively at the tea leaves.

"You are unmarried," she said.

The Detective-Sergeant looked in astonishment at Dr. Johns.

She turned the cup around in her hand and peeped into it. "I see a large H."

She looked again.

"You do a considerable amount of inspection work in regard to your job."

Something worried her. She held the cup up against the light and looked fleetingly at Detective-Sergeant Demosthenes H. de Goede.

"There's an unpleasant task ahead of you. I see a very big man in your future and you will have a lot to do with him. I see the letters A.K.S."

She shook out some of the tea leaves and turned the cup around and around.

"I see a crown. You are going to have considerable success in your work. Your health is good. You are shortly going overseas. There's a letter for you."

She frowned.

"There's a lot of tea leaves here widely dispersed. This is extremely unusual. You get around a good deal, don't you?"

She shook the cup and closed her eyes wearily.

"I have been very busy today," she said to Dr. Johns. "Three groups of visitors and eminent guests have been here today. I hardly knew where to turn."

She looked into the cup again.

"There's a warning sign." She showed Detective-Sergeant Demosthenes H. de Goede a thick pile of tea leaves. "But I can't quite make out what it means. Be careful. I see you do not easily allow yourself to be influenced, but be careful all the same before you come to a decision. There are many who look up to you."

Suddenly she sniffed.

"I smell burning," she said to Dr. Johns.

She was about to jump up and go to the kitchen when she saw the column of smoke through the window. She became agitated all over again.

"Everything is in order," Dr. Johns comforted her. "Everything is under control."

"Eighteen years ago I was raped," she said to Dr. Johns. "I thought things like that belonged to the past."

"Everything is under control," said Dr. Johns.

She looked uneasily into the cup.

"Someone has died," she said to Detective-Sergeant Demosthenes H. de Goede. "But not a relation of yours. Nevertheless, the death of this person affects you. I see the letter L."

She shook out more tea leaves.

"I see a big reception with many people, in the near future. Important things will happen there. I see something that flies. It looks like a large bat. Be careful. I see a fight or a big conflict, but the right party will win. One day you will inherit a lot of money. Are there any questions?"

She looked at her watch.

"You have two questions and one wish," said Dr. Johns in a whisper to Detective-Sergeant Demosthenes H. de Goede.

Detective-Sergeant Demosthenes H. de Goede thought for a moment and then stuttered anxiously. "Are his hands strong enough for karate or must he confine himself to judo?" asked Dr. Johns.

Mrs. Dreyer looked at him in amazement and then took refuge in the cup.

"Yes," she said.

Detective-Sergeant Demosthenes H. de Goede was at once ready with his other question.

"Must he concentrate on the further development of the *latissimus dorsi*, or should he rather devote his attention to the regulation of the central abdominal belt?"

"No," said Mrs. Dreyer.

She put the cup back in the saucer and waited with closed eyes.

"The wish," Dr. Johns whispered.

Detective-Sergeant Demosthenes H. de Goede frowned with thought and then relaxed as he formulated his wish to himself.

"Your wish will be fulfilled," said Mrs. Dreyer and stood up. She peered out of the window and opened the curtains.

"I saw something remarkable this afternoon," she said over her shoulder to Dr. Johns and looked up into the sky. "I could have sworn I saw a man flying through the air." She turned her back to the window and walked back into the middle of the room. "But perhaps it is because I am so overworked. Imagine: *three* groups of visitors in succession. I have not enough tea left for supper." She shook hands with Detective-Sergeant Demosthenes H. de Goede when she saw the money on the table. "Of course, it could have been a large bird," she said pensively. She walked ahead of them down the passage to the front door and saw the smoke column from another angle.

"Are you sure, Doctor Johns, that we will not have a repetition of eighteen years ago?"

Dr. Johns shook his head.

She went out of the door into the garden. She bent to pick a few dead flowers.

"When did you last see Jock Silberstein, Doctor Johns?"

"We have just seen him," said Dr. Johns. "These days he has withdrawn from everything and actually is interested only in Adam Kadmon Silberstein."

Mrs. Dreyer turned on a tap and began to water the garden with a hose.

"You must tell him that he must not so easily forget his old friends, Doctor Johns." She straightened her hair with her hand. "It's months since I saw him."

"That's true," said Dr. Johns. "He ought to get around more. It doesn't do him any good to concern himself all the time with the Giant."

Mrs. Dreyer waved to them from the garden gate.

Detective-Sergeant Demosthenes H. de Goede was scarlet with excitement. He could hardly wait to be alone with Dr. Johns. He stuttered so rapidly that even Dr. Johns found it difficult to follow him.

"Yes," said Dr. Johns. "Remarkable woman. She has a special gift."

They walked considerably faster as the sun began to sink quickly and the clouds take on definite gradations of red.

The light fell, too, on Detective-Sergeant Demosthenes H. de Goede whose face, scarlet with excitement and reflected light, was painfully distorted in his effort to formulate to himself, once again, the events of the past half hour.

"You know," said Dr. Johns to Detective-Sergeant Demosthenes H. de Goede as they walked through the heather toward the next hill, "I am thinking again of our earlier conversation today when we spoke about the mythological conflict between the gods and the Giants. The conflict was grotesquely comic. One knows with absolute certainty that the Olympian gods should win, but every time one of the gods wounds a Giant, Hercules has to finish him off."

Dr. Johns reveled in having found someone who had so intense an interest in this subject. It was remarkable how thoroughly young people were educated these days.

"As you know, there were twenty-four Giants," said Dr. Johns, "but I know the names of only a few." He reflected, the heather brushing damply against them, the herbal fragrance of the veld filling the surroundings. "I know that Alcyoneus was the leader of the Giants. His nickname was The Mighty Ass. They say he was perhaps the soul of the sirocco. The burning breath of the wild ass that starts nightmares and incites man to murder and rape."

A group of guests, eminent visitors, residents and relatives, led by a tired guide, struggled past them through the heather. Madam Ritchie and her two daughters were way behind, and they waved lustily to Detective-Sergeant Demosthenes H. de Goede, who was prevented by Dr. Johns from joining them. Hope's and Prudence's hair hung in ragged strands around their shoulders and they looked like wild daughters of nature.

"And then, of course, there was Porphyrion," said Dr. Johns, "who, at the moment of attacking Hera, was wounded by an arrow from Eros' bow. The terrible pain changed to lust, he wrenched her beautiful cloak from her and exposed her in her glorious nakedness — and Hercules killed him."

A second group of residents, guests and eminent visitors appeared from another direction. It seemed as if they were trying to catch up with the first group: proteas and harebells were trodden flat as they struggled through the mud. The guide, well ahead, repeatedly looked at his watch and encouraged them enthusiastically. A single, dejected figure was about to drop out.

"Pallas, the erotic, wished to dishonor his own daughter, Pallas Athena; she knocked him to the ground with a stone — and Hercules killed him."

Dr. Johns looked curiously at the dejected figure sitting alone among the heather.

"Ephialtes fought Aries, Apollo shot him in the left eye. Hercules passed and shot him in the right eye — and killed him."

The dejected figure looked longingly at them. He plucked a protea hopelessly and threw it away. His torso was naked and he was blue with cold.

"Klutios was burned by Hecate with burning brands — and Hercules killed him."

The dejected figure had his toes in the mud and messed around in it like an impatient child. His trousers were sopping and his beard full of pollen. He looked with tear-filled eyes at Dr. Johns and Detective-Sergeant Demosthenes H. de Goede, who stopped close beside him.

"Eurytus was felled by Dionysus with his Bacchus-staff — and Hercules killed him."

The dejected figure suddenly jumped up and took up a position, legs wide apart, right in their path, his arms on his hips, his body dripping with moisture from the heather.

"Where can I go?" he asked furiously. "Is there no place where I can find shelter? And hot food and clothes?" He swung his arms. "Every time I join up with people they take me to factories and lectures. Nobody concerns himself with me. Is that Christian?" He was so furious he could hardly speak.

Dr. Johns and Detective-Sergeant Demosthenes H. de Goede looked with interest at the enraged figure.

"The place is very crowded with all the guests and eminent visitors," said Dr. Johns. "The rain spoiled everything and the funeral was, of course, an unexpected event. One can actually not blame anyone. Tremendous organization is attached to all the proceedings." He rubbed his chin and suddenly came to a decision. He pointed toward the cottages that he and Detective-Sergeant Demosthenes H. de Goede had just left. "Go and ask at one of them. Someone will quite possibly have room for you."

The furious figure had in the meantime calmed down and was doing his best to regain his dignity. Dripping, he bowed to Dr. Johns and walked with sucking sounds through the mud toward a cottage in the distance.

"Hephaistos burned the giant Mimas with a red-hot iron," said Dr. Johns as he and Detective-Sergeant Demosthenes H. de Goede wandered on, " — and Hercules killed him."

They moved faster, since the sun was low on the horizon and the first houses with asbestos roofs gleamed in the distance.

"It makes one feel sad," said Dr. Johns. "Our little walk is fast coming to an end and," he smiled at Detective-Sergeant Demosthenes H. de Goede, "I can't thank you enough for your enlightened and pleasant company."

Detective-Sergeant Demosthenes H. de Goede stuttered modestly.

Dr. Johns blew his nose.

"It really was pleasant, and I hope that one day, when your task is done, you will again visit us as a guest of the Foundation."

They had now come right up to the little houses with asbestos roofs and stood for a moment to admire the scene. The spotless white houses stood in a row, each with a square of garden in front and a lavatory behind. The red of the sunset tinted the walls with all shades of red. It was a restful scene, a true evening scene.

"That little house in the middle," said Dr. Johns, "belonged to the gardener, the grandfather of the white-faced girl, the great-grandfather of Lila who was murdered."

They began to walk slowly toward the house.

"Eighteen years ago these were all houses of ill fame," said Dr. Johns and smiled at Detective-Sergeant Demosthenes H. de Goede who blushed. "But they no longer fulfill that function. In fact, such places have become an anachronism, because that particular satisfaction is these days obtained in society itself, with the enlightened cooperation of women of all classes." He blew his nose again and fastened his jacket. He looked rather anxious and popped a little pill into his mouth. "I think we can say with pride that we have deprived sex of its secretiveness and made it commonplace."

They were now in front of the house and a gay little scene greeted them. The uncle from Welkom stood in the door, the uncle from the Karroo was working in the garden, the old woman with silver hair and the girl who looked like a little sow were each peeping out of a window.

"Welcome!" said the uncle from Welkom.

He had the dignity of one who is not only head of a family, but of an entire dynasty.

"Come in," he said, "and enjoy a cup of tea."

All four of them had taken over the house and moved about as if they had been at home there for years. The old woman and the girl were both busy knitting with clicking needles and wool of a garish color.

"We found them in one of the cupboards," said the old woman with silver hair.

"We found the oddest articles of clothing," said the girl who looked like a little sow. She named them, except the unmentionable, which she had herself put on. It was clear that the clothes of their only niece had already been divided among them.

The uncle from the Karroo wanted to know in whose name the house had been transferred. Had Lila perhaps inherited it from her grandfather?

"It belongs to the farm," said Dr. Johns as he blew his tea cool. "It is part of the Foundation."

The uncle from the Karroo knocked out his pipe on his shoe.

"Have you perhaps seen the will and the deed of transfer?" he asked Dr. Johns.

The uncle from Welkom interrupted him.

"We won't bother Doctor Johns with such problems now,"

he said. "We can hold them over until a later and more appropriate time."

"When the pain is past," said the old woman with silver hair.

The girl who looked like a little sow began to cry softly.

A corn-cricket walked across the floor and disappeared toward the kitchen, as everyone watched it anxiously.

"*Eugaster longipes*," said Dr. Johns.

"The place needs a thorough cleaning," said the uncle from the Karroo.

"Tomorrow is another day," said the uncle from Welkom.

They drank tea in silence and then the uncle from Welkom said with a sigh: "So, it was here that our beloved niece, Lila, spent her last years. I hope everyone was kind to her."

The uncle from the Karroo lit his pipe again.

"Tell me, Doctor Johns, is Mr. Silberstein a Jew?"

Dr. Johns put his empty cup down on the table and nodded.

The aunt nudged the girl, and the uncle from the Karroo drew deeply on his pipe.

"And the Giant, Adam Kadmon Silberstein," asked the uncle from Welkom, "is he a Jew, Doctor Johns?"

Dr. Johns shrugged.

"Sort of half and half."

The uncle from the Karroo and the uncle from Welkom looked meaningfully at one another. The old woman with silver hair and the girl who looked like a little sow kept their eyes fixed on their knitting.

"Our niece, Lila, was raped, was she not?" the uncle from Welkom asked in a soft voice.

"We are not quite sure," began Dr. Johns, but the uncle from Welkom stopped him and pointed to the old woman and the girl, who had stopped knitting and covered their faces with their hands. The girl who looked like a little sow suddenly got up and walked quickly from the room, her dress swaying and the last souvenir of Lila shining colorfully in the twilight.

The face of the uncle from the Karroo was hard.

"The unholy alliance!" he said suddenly. "The foul conspiracy!" He turned to Detective-Sergeant Demosthenes H. de Goede. "We trust in you, Sergeant," he said hotly.

The uncle from Welkom whispered something to him. They both stood up. The aunt with silver hair made her farewells with a limp hand of grief and went to the kitchen to prepare the evening meal. A suppressed scream signified her second meeting with the corn-cricket and then they could all hear the scraping of a broom and the opening and closing of the back door.

At the garden gate the uncle from the Karroo said to Detective-Sergeant Demosthenes H. de Goede: "There are rumors, Sergeant, about a giant, that our beloved Lila was . . ." but the uncle from Welkom stopped him.

"I think the Sergeant and I understand each other," he said.

Detective-Sergeant Demosthenes H. de Goede and Dr. Johns left the house with the asbestos roof, while the two uncles leaned over the hedge and looked fixedly up at the sky as if they espied the possibility of more rain.

"I tell you it was a vulture," said the uncle from Welkom emphatically.

"It was an omen," said the uncle from the Karroo equally emphatically. "We often see them in the Karroo."

The uncle from Welkom silenced him and gave a last wave to Dr. Johns and Detective-Sergeant Demosthenes H. de Goede. The last rays of the sun glowed on the house and painted the doors and blinds, which were being firmly bolted for the coming night.

walked slowly through the heather and saw
Welgevonden at its most beautiful. A single poplar was a burning monolith against the horizon.

"There is the trout lake," said Dr. Johns and pointed to a sheet of water that lay calm as a mirror under the slope of the mountain. A fleet of boats with their load of residents, guests and eminent visitors were congregating from far and wide at the wharf. The weeping masks drew a line of marble down to the fountain above the Welgevonden houses. The water moved in a shining stream, shot through the mouths like fountains and glittered with every imaginable color. And all along the line of water the tired guests moved without their guides: a slow, lazy movement toward the buildings that waited among the trees.

"After tonight," said Dr. Johns with a touch of sadness in his voice, "I shall have to leave you. My particular task will have been completed."

They were moving down, past the trout lake, past the Corinthian columns reflected in the water, along the masks on the winding way of the stream.

"I am an old man," said Dr. Johns. "I have passed the stage when I aspire to build up a definite personality. I am actually also past the stage of really taking an interest in individuals. I am curious only about the broad characteristics. If I die tomorrow, or the next day, I want the complete view only." He was silent for a moment. "But even that is no longer so important."

Detective-Sergeant Demosthenes H. de Goede made a gesture of dissent.

Along the road they met Henry Silberstein-van Eeden. He nodded briefly to Detective-Sergeant Demosthenes H. de Goede and turned to Dr. Johns.

"I have thought about it," he said, excited. "I have realized that everywhere here I have freedom: in the Foundation, in the research offices, among the residents, in the laboratories." He sought for the right words. "The freedom of specialized niches: the small areas in which one can realize oneself."

Dr. Johns smiled and did his best to give his face an expression of venerable wisdom, but all he could achieve was a wrinkled look of cunning.

"It's a feeling of being alone that drives one to the Foundation," said Henry. "Yearning and loneliness. It is not *what* happens here, but the possibility that something revealing *will* happen, that here one will get away from the uncomprehensive abstraction of the world within one." He still sought in vain for the right words in which to express his insight.

"And so the Foundation must be protected at all costs?" asked Dr. Johns and winked at Detective-Sergeant Demosthenes H. de Goede.

But Henry walked on alone, unwilling at that stage to think about the most important consequence.

"They all come here," said Dr. Johns, "in proportion as the Promethean guilt accumulates out there. Bomb-shocked victims of the explosions in themselves."

Dr. Johns and Detective-Sergeant Demosthenes H. de Goede greeted Madam Ritchie and her two daughters. They had brought their hair under control by tying it with red and blue ribbons from Mon Repos. Hope and Prudence ran to Detective-Sergeant Demosthenes H. de Goede like tall, slim daughters and embraced him. He looked with beaming face from one to the other and then his eyes grew serious as he tried, for the hundredth time, to decide on the particular status of each, resident or relative. Each felt equally soft, each was equally warm and the chatter of each was equally vapid. But Madam Ritchie was in a hurry: supper had still to be prepared, they had all to go to bed early because there was a long day and a great occasion ahead tomorrow. Mr. de Goede was always welcome, however.

The two girls tore themselves away and waved gaily to him as they frisked off after their corpulent mother with ponytails and red and blue ribbons swaying.

"Everyone on Welgevonden," said Dr. Johns, "follows his own illusions undisturbed. It is not that there is something here that the outside world hasn't got, it's just that everything happens more slowly, that it is a small order inside a big order." He tried to think of an example. "It's like an enormous theater where everyone assembles — not to do anything, but to see a completed film."

They greeted the universally-liked Dries, who walked hurriedly past them; he raised his hat. There was an ecstatic smile on his face. He looked frequently up into the air and his shining eyes reflected the aftermath of his vision. An improved breeding policy was already emergent, a sort of matriarchy with the bull's strain kept to a minimum, with the bull features broken down to the elemental, strictly controlled act of artificial insemination — that was the prophetic idea of Uncle Giepie, that was his triumph over the monster, that was the vision blessed by the figure in the clouds. He walked faster. Deep down inside him, half formed but genuine and true, the policy was growing — that he could feel, in his entire being.

"We can simply learn to live with what there is," said Dr. Johns. "We can only hope that an empty ritual will again become meaningful."

He bowed to one of the eminent guests.

"If only we could find something great," sighed Dr. Johns. "But we are actually only a parody of the outside world. We differ only in that we provide a buffer for every resident. We protect fantasy when it clashes with reality, we protect the image of reality when it clashes with the fantasy of the time."

They became aware of someone beside one of the masks: a shivering figure who hid himself behind the gushing maw until all the guests and visitors had passed. It was a shivering figure that made not the slightest attempt to attract attention or to ask for help. He simply sat with his back to the mask and his feet in the water that rushed noisily from the maw. His trousers were soaked, his torso was marked with red blotches, as if boiling water had fallen on him.

He did not at first answer when Dr. Johns spoke to him. Then he said dolefully: "She threw boiling tea over me. She said I was a barbarian who wished to rape her, and then she threw the boiling tea over me."

He no longer tried to maintain his dignity. He had given up the struggle: he even felt strangely at home at Welgevonden, where he was treated so cavalierly.

"I was covered with tea leaves," said the shivering figure. "And do you imagine that she tried to help me?" Indignation strove unsuccessfully to get the upper hand, then subsided beneath this peaceful fatalism. "She stood before me, that fat little woman in her heathen dress, and she began telling my fortune. A witch of Endor!" He held his feet up to the stream of water and watched it spurt between his toes. "She sees prison walls and the hand of justice. She sees the horsemen of the Apocalypse!" He paddled his feet in the stream. His chin was sunk on his chest and he seemed to be looking at his navel. He had already forgotten Dr. Johns, in his shivering contemplation of the world.

"And this is the fountain," said Dr. Johns a moment later as they passed the last mask and looked between the statues at the lily-covered surface. "It's particularly high, the water is boisterous, the cement pipes can't cope with carrying away the water to the industrial installations."

The plastic swans swayed to and fro as if they had landed on a sea. Often the waves toppled a swan and then it reappeared a little way off, straight again.

"It's here that Jock Silberstein found Lila," said Dr. Johns.

All the visitors, eminent guests and residents had disappeared already in the direction of Welgevonden's houses. The sun was behind the mountain and the evening shadows were purple.

Detective-Sergeant Demosthenes H. de Goede looked at the grass around the fountain, but it was flattened by hundreds of feet. He was looking around for clues and found all sorts of garments and personal articles that had been lost. In the end he found a single line of unusual footprints. He knelt next to them and made notes busily in his notebook. According to their measurements, they must have been the footprints of a colossal person. When he did his calculations later that night, he would be able to determine the exact height and weight of the gigantic figure.

Entirely satisfied, he joined Dr. Johns and they strolled lazily over the lawn to one of the glass houses that had been assigned him as his quarters for the duration of his visit. On the way they came across Jock Silberstein and Adam Kadmon Silberstein. The Giant was still being obstinate, but was firmly led by its hand.

"It's time for young boys to go home," said Jock Silberstein and smiled at the Giant, who wore the scarlet ribbon of Mon Repos around his neck. "Early to bed and early to rise, makes Adam Kadmon healthy and wise."

At his own glass house, the nearest to the fountain, Dr. Johns had to take his leave.

"And I, too, must go home," said Jock Silberstein. "Like Cronus, I am banished to the Golden Age and to the Blessed Island." He pointed to the house of Welgevonden among the battling trees. The cumbersome figure of the Giant and the slightly crooked, tall man constituted an extraordinary pair as they walked away and for the last time left Dr. Johns and Detective-Sergeant Demosthenes H. de Goede alone.

Dr. Johns stood at the door of the glass house, a slight little man in the twilight.

"I hope I was helpful," he said eagerly.

Detective-Sergeant Demosthenes H. de Goede stuttered a protest against the modesty of his conductor.

"I hope I did not influence you in any way." Dr. Johns folded his hands piously and looked after Jock Silberstein and the Giant on their way to the Big House. "It would upset me very much if I were to discover that I exercised any influence in any way upon you and your detective work."

Detective-Sergeant Demosthenes H. de Goede repeated his protest proudly.

Dr. Johns' face brightened suddenly.

"One can say that I perhaps filled the role of a sort of present-day Meturgeman. I, too, merely formulated certain obscure aspects of the situation and summed them up in understandable language, not so?"

He unlocked the door and switched on the lights. Coincidentally, at that very moment, lights went on in many other glass rooms as well, as the guests, residents and dignitaries reached their rooms.

"I concede that I sometimes went so far as to play the role of exegete," said Dr. Johns reflectively.

Detective-Sergeant Demosthenes H. de Goede looked in amazement at the people who were undressing and, visible to one another, doing the most intimate things in their glass rooms.

"The rooms were specially designed for observation from outside," said Dr. Johns. "The relatives, guests and eminent visitors must naturally adapt themselves to the Foundation, where everything is designed in the interests of the residents. You'd be surprised how quickly one becomes accustomed to it."

Dr. Johns suddenly stretched out his hand and greeted Detective-Sergeant Demosthenes H. de Goede ceremoniously. He still had the *ephialtion* in his other hand. Perhaps Detective-Sergeant Demosthenes H. de Goede would take it along? An exceptionally rare plant with certain magical properties, according to tradition.

Detective-Sergeant Demosthenes H. de Goede demonstrated, as so often before, his remarkable memory by stuttering a reminder to Dr. Johns of his intention to . . . well . . . undertake certain . . . excavations.

Dr. Johns expressed his surprise at the Detective-Sergeant's retentive memory and reassured him that he, Dr. Johns, still had every intention of carrying out his intention; but that the Detective-Sergeant could naturally have no official knowledge of this, in view of there being no warrant which, in the nature of the weather conditions, was unobtainable. The result of the investigation would, however, be made known to him in due course.

He greeted the Detective-Sergeant a second time and went into his room. His movements, although they could still see each other clearly, underwent the subtle transformation of someone alone and invisible to another.

Detective-Sergeant Demosthenes H. de Goede walked slowly to his room, gaping as he went at the guests and eminent visitors who exposed themselves in the most intimate manner, apparently suffering from the same illusion as fish in an aquarium that the darkness outside, because of the light inside, enclosed them in a separate world. He lingered for a while at the Swedish lady's glass room and then entered his own room, where he at once became the victim of the same illusion when he switched on his light.

He undressed quickly, ate a few sandwiches that he took from his little tin trunk and got comfortably into bed. He took out his notebook, uncapped his fountain pen, and wrote: "Just like fishes in an aquarium, mankind suffers from the illusion that he is invisible." It would later form the nucleus of a poem in *The Police Officer*. Presently it occurred to him that he had not yet done his before-bed exercises, but he decided to forego them, since he had been particularly active all day. He noticed the plant on the bedside table, smelled it, put it back and switched out the light. With hands folded behind his head, peaceful against the pillows, he could see clearly in the dark the lighted glass room next door, where the Swedish lady, under the general illusion of invisibility, was doing a striptease. It looked so genuine that after a while he even began to wonder whether, maybe, she were not enticing him in the most shameless manner. Later, he began worrying all over again because he had not done his bedtime exercises. Fortunately, there were also isometric exercises that one could do lying on one's back. His breathing grew more rapid and his body stiffened in the complicated process.

Thereafter he relaxed and drifted into a dreamless sleep with the *ephialtion* near his head.

QUIBUS AUXILIIS?

that was soft. There was the passion of abandonment. There was the very first night, the whisper of her dress and her pale face. She bent over him, her teeth gleamed and she slavered over him. There were games with someone with black eyes and suddenly it was dark. There was something warm soft against him. He fought back, winning and losing simultaneously. He drank from the white breasts. He caught a little bird and wrung its neck. The creature lay fluttering on the ground and expired in its own blood. Someone came from behind and he felt something soft. His hand was wet. The waters splashed over him. The masks roared and everything was cold. He felt strong again. Suddenly he was weak. His life was draining from him. He strangled her but his hands grew numb. He tried to strangle her but she bit him on the left side of his throat and he felt the warm blood. Once, he had lain in soft arms and soft hands had caressed him. He grew strong and wished to destroy the softness. On other days he longed for it. Where were the dark eyes? She appeared among the curtains and her breath smelled of blood. She asked him to kill her. She whispered something in his ear and he throttled her, but his hands grew slack. Where was she lying? She was everywhere. She rushed down on him and he struck her away from him. His hands sank into her body. And suddenly she was no longer there. He looked up into the black eyes and saw the enormous breasts. The breasts were big and the nipples black and pointed. He wept suddenly and was filled with longing for something that he could not understand. He could destroy everyone if he wished, but he suddenly felt weak. Someone must stroke him. He

waited and saw something by the curtains. Sometimes he remembered the name Salome, but she said Lila! — Lila! she
screamed, and then he faded away. The door was locked. The
moon shone through the window. The fountain roared.
Those faces roared. He wanted to sleep, but he could not
sleep. The large man came and took his hand. His hand was
rough and strong. And there, suddenly, was she! But they
locked him in. The key grated in the lock and he lay straight
on the bed. He stretched. His feet protruded from the blankets. He felt cold. There was something warm on him. A
sharp pain. Her voice was soft and lovely. Do this! she said.
Do this! she ordered. Why did nothing happen? He waited
and waited and waited, and nothing happened. He called her
name and nothing happened. He lay and waited, and watched
the curtains. There were baubles in her hair. Her hair hung
down on either side of her face. She laughed with sharp teeth.
Come! she said and the curtains waved. She always said
Come! and then she was gone. And suddenly she was there
again. Something bit him and he felt exhausted. But then
he felt strong again. Someone hurt him. He wept and someone comforted him. She was so small that one could bend her
in two. Harder! she screamed and was suddenly gone. He
wished to sleep but he could not sleep. Where was she? The
curtains moved but it was not she. Where is Lila? he asked and
the man took his hand. His hand was rough and big. Nothing
happened. The curtains swayed and swayed and there, suddenly, she was, but suddenly she was no longer there. He
wanted to bite something but everything was tough and there
was no blood. Bite! she screamed. But there was nothing to

a drugged semblance of death and dreamed dreams that she would not remember the next morning.

In the glass room next door Prudence slept surrounded by photographs of film stars. Her hair had been brushed three hundred times, her arms hung down on either side of the bed and the tips of her fingers touched the floor. Her young breasts swelled under the transparent nylon, a spider's web created under the trade name Vanity Fair; she needed no pills, her blood was warm and her skin soft. She lay relaxed on her back, exposed receptively in a condition of dreamless sleep.

In the third glass room Hope lay naked on a blanketless bed. Her hair, too, had been brushed three hundred times and lay in soft folds on either side of her face. Her body was full and young and exposed to the night. Her eyes were open and her lips moist: shameless wishful images thronged her distorted mind and became visible in the moonlight in the movements of her limbs, her restless hands and the erotic undulations of her whole body. This was the "resting" image of the tormented resident; the pitiful nymphomaniac who suffered in solitude continual unsatisfaction; whose impotence was understood by nobody; who with frequent coitus would remain always sterile. All her movements in that half-sleep were a parody of provocation and satisfaction, a continual repetition of Satanic sterility, a witchdom between glass windows, and an eternal suffering on the pyre of the ceaseless fire in herself.)

The curtains moved and someone was in the room. There was a dark figure before the window. Chunky and dark against the moon. Black John with his cold sword. You lay .

still and nothing happened. You heard the movement and
rolled toward it and you knew then in that taunting moment
that nothing would happen. But it was the old thing: the ballet
of hesitation. The moon shone through the window and still
you could see nothing. But he was there. Black John was invisible in the shadows of the moon; there was no reflection
of him in the mirror. You stretched out in sensual invitation,
you spread yourself out in a position of maximum receptivity.
You awaited the hated contact and you felt that you could
wait no longer. You twisted your fingers through your hair
and ran your fingers over your skin. It was a matter of time
and then you heard the slight shuffle and waited for the en-
suing silence. It was a creative urge that could never be stilled,
but you obtained a limited satisfaction in the creative movement, although there was no satisfaction. Something very
close to you moved and you answered with swelling breasts.
There was a dragging sound and you stretched in thrilling sus-
pense. Something touched the bed and you became soft with
receptivity. You awaited first the hand that would touch
here, there, everywhere — but you knew it would not happen
at once. You awaited your lover in the dark with all the darkness in yourself. You repeated the dark ritual mechanically
and waited for the mechanical contact. There was no end to
the unbearable repetition; there was no consummation of the
aching wish. You found your substitute satisfaction in the act
that had no end, in the repetition that would lead to nothing.
You lived only for the movement without expectation that
you would ever be carried to your destination.

And then you felt the hand assaulting your breasts. You

heard and felt the presence that would destroy you. You felt the destruction as the heavy weight flattened your little mattress against the springs. You were compelled to play the part of a fugitive in the flight that *had* to satisfy you. (Even though you knew it could not happen.) You suffered the semblance of being overwhelmed, but you really felt overpowered. You felt the teeth in your throat and screamed with a pain you hated and welcomed. In the passion of your creativity you knew that creation would never be achieved. You clamored yieldingly and fought compliantly. You were tortured by the welcome assault. You felt the hot blood that stirred your revulsion. You spurred destruction on; you whispered the death wish with a banality that came not from yourself. You surrendered with murderous fury. And then you muttered the name in imitation of the eventual satisfaction that you did not feel.

You named your desire . . . Jock, Henry.

Named all the names of acquaintances and strangers and named in vain the names that would exorcise evil by love, and would save yourself. Named even Adam Kadmon with his clumsy body. Called in vain to everyone you hated. Spoke the name of the young hero. Named the athletic, half-godlike figure. Muttered and called the name until all had passed and, wide awake, you took your revenge and sent one shriek of dissatisfaction after the other into the night. You screamed your fury in the moonlit night and found your satisfaction in all the lights you caused to spring up, in the glass houses that caught fire, and the noise in the night.

You heard the monster, satiated, fleeing. You welcomed

the light in your room. You found your satisfaction in the anxious faces of your dearest. You came nearest to complete satisfaction through the anxiety and rage of those who loved you. You burned, then, on the glorious pyre. You became suddenly visible in the role of the holy virgin.

EXHUMATIO

(While the screams rent the night, the lights jerked on one after another. Moonlight was replaced by electric light and the tableau was continued in the numerous glass rooms. The residents, guests and eminent visitors looked repeatedly at one another; they jumped out of bed and exposed themselves to one another in all the colorfulness of their intimate nightwear: the men in striped pajamas, the women in transparent pink and white material.

Madam Ritchie stumbled through to Prudence's room, she and Prudence burst into Hope's room and fell on their knees next to the bed from which the naked girl screamed lustily. They looked at the open window and saw the moving curtains. Then they joined her and screamed inordinately for help from the rest of the Foundation.

In the glass rooms there was great activity. The residents, guests and eminent visitors hastily donned their dressing gowns and ran outside. In the bright light from the glass windows they met one another coming from all directions. There was such turmoil that the unknown miscreant could automatically disappear merely by standing still and becoming part of the crowd. They crowded around the blue glass house and saw Madam Ritchie throw a transparent gown over her naked daughter. Then she opened the door to them and they streamed in as if they had not seen enough. The two daughters became the object of their attention. They were quickly over-whelmed in the mass and, as more and more arrived, could scarcely move. Presently they filled the adjoining rooms and made the glass house hum with the force of their speculations. They no longer knew whether Hope or Prudence had been the victim and each of them had already arrived at his own decision and disseminated his own rumor. Hope and Pru-dence were both in tears; both, like the crowd, in dressing gowns; they were both sipping brandy that was being offered them. Most of the residents and guests could not get into the rooms and returned to their own rooms where they made coffee and continued their speculations, watching each other through the windows. The reappearance of the evildoer had completed the expected pattern. Lila's name was added to Hope's and Prudence's. The extent of the threat had increased — they all felt intimately concerned. Revenge and retribu-tion were now really on campaign. The ranks of the com-munity were closed.

The lights burned in all the glass houses except one: Detec-tive-Sergeant Demosthenes H. de Goede's, who in dreamless sleep enjoyed his night's rest.

After an hour or two the noise and turmoil decreased — a point of satiety had been reached. The rooms emptied and Madam Ritchie, Hope and Prudence locked themselves se-curely in one room. One by one the lights went out and keys grated in locks. The moonlight regained its supremacy and shone softly silver on the shut glass.)

Somewhere on Welgevonden, in a cemetery beneath the moon,

as everyone slept once again, a lively presentation of an old legend was revived. It was as if Dr. John Dee and Edward Kelly stood again within the double circle amid the planetary symbols and the names of Raphael, Rael and Tarniel. Beside an open grave it was as if the two magicians were again in consultation with a ghostly apparition in a shroud, and were asking for an answer about the future.

In the moonlight everything was delusive. It could have been the recreation of an old Jewish custom, according to Rabbi Manassah: that the dead would return for a year, that one could make an invocation to them, as the witch of Endor to the dead prophet Samuel, and that a light on the future could be obtained.

In that moonlight landscape it could also have been a scene from the Middle Ages where someone (dressed like that little figure in the dark cloak) wished to render evil harmless with a single stab of a holy aspen staff.

It could also have been of the modern time as, by way of distorting the past, the scientist brought the dead back to obtain, by means of investigation and dissection, an answer to his despair.

Those who had suffered a violent death were seldom left undisturbed if they bothered the community. By different incantations, alternating from age-old formulas of exorcism to the officialese of warrants, they were dissected for the sake of the peace of all.

In the moonlight, around the grave, by the light of a lantern, the process was repeated. And in the distance, beyond the light but visible nevertheless, was a giant figure that watched everything quietly.

QUOMODO?

QUOMODO? · 1 · When Detective-Sergeant Demosthenes H. de Goede awoke the next morning he found Judge O'Hara at his door. The old man in his black toga, gray with dust, nodded amiably, placed his staff in a corner of the room and sat down on a chair. With a movement of his hand he granted the Detective-Sergeant permission to do his physical exercises.

The curtains of the neighboring glass rooms were drawn, since it was now daytime and a good many residents, guests and eminent visitors were watching with interest the Detective-Sergeant who was warming up before doing more complicated movements. This compelled him to draw his own curtains, because of the small crowd that had gathered in front of his window.

"Greetings from Doctor Johns," said Judge O'Hara. "He can unfortunately not be here today." He shook with a soundless fit of laughter. "He asked me, however, to inform you that the necessary investigation was made last night."

Detective-Sergeant Demosthenes H. de Goede, involved in freehand exercises, stuttered a question.

"I can't hear a word," said Judge O'Hara.

Detective-Sergeant Demosthenes H. de Goede repeated his stuttered question.

Judge O'Hara found the repeated question equally incomprehensible.

"Write it down, man," he said.

Detective-Sergeant Demosthenes H. de Goede wrote neatly on a piece of paper: "What were Dr. Johns' findings?"

"Exactly what he expected," said Judge O'Hara impatiently. He looked around the room, saw the small plant beside the bed and nodded his satisfaction. "I see you made provision for a good night's rest. Pity Hope and Prudence didn't have one too."

Detective-Sergeant Demosthenes H. de Goede was completely in the dark and wished to write down another question, but Judge O'Hara ordered him to finish his exercises and to dress.

"I gather from Doctor Johns that, in the nature of things, he is interested in the mythological parallel to your mission. Early this morning I did some research and found something in Aristophanes that will certainly interest you. Verse 1039 of Rogers' translation of his well-known work, where the monster Typhon, against whom Hercules is fighting, is described: 'And [it had] a *lamia's* groin . . .' " He looked triumphantly at Detective-Sergeant Demosthenes H. de Goede, who had just finished his exercises. He was, however, obviously disappointed at the Detective-Sergeant's lack of enthusiasm.

"*Lamia* . . ." he repeated and watched with barely concealed dissatisfaction as the Detective-Sergeant dressed himself in brand new sports clothes which he had just taken from his little trunk. "Perhaps you know the expression *empusa* better." He looked expectantly up. "It's a variant of the *lamia* and Rogers uses the word 'vampires' in his translation of the *Ranae*." He sat back cosily to enjoy the Detective-Sergeant's shock of interest. When there was still no reaction, he suddenly came under the influence of the policeman's iron self-discipline. "It's at any rate interesting to know that Hercules also fought against a vampire," he said forlornly.

Detective-Sergeant Demosthenes H. de Goede listened courteously, but he seemed to be confining his attention to a tie (in the colors of the police college) which he was tying in an Edwardian knot.

"Naturally I realize," said Judge O'Hara, "that a more complete understanding of vampires really came into being under Slavic influence, but all the same there are enough indications of their existence in the time of Hadrian. The case mentioned by Phlegon of Tralles, for instance." He peeped expectantly at Detective-Sergeant Demosthenes H. de Goede, who had just put on an old boy's blazer. "The case of Machates, who slept with the erotic vampire, Philinnion."

The Detective-Sergeant was busy combing his hair and deepening the waves with the palm of his hand.

"I assume that it is unnecessary to refer to Menippos' bride, who united the arts of Aphrodite with her lust for blood."

Judge O'Hara laughed heartily with Detective-Sergeant Demosthenes H. de Goede who, exquisitely dressed, was a paragon of youthful virility. There really *was* something attractive about this young man. Dr. Johns was right. A pity though that he suffered from a speech defect. Judge O'Hara helpfully pushed the paper and pencil nearer.

"I hope you all had a good night's rest," wrote Detective-Sergeant Demosthenes H. de Goede.

Judge O'Hara could hardly contain his feeling of amazement.

"Did you not hear? Hope or Prudence was violated last night by a gigantic vampire!"

Now he was pleasantly surprised by the Detective-Sergeant's unexpected reaction, as he wrenched open the door and ran outside in the direction of the blue glass house.

Judge O'Hara first took up his staff from beside the bed and then, slow and content, followed along the path to Hope's and Prudence's glass room.

2

They were welcomed by a melancholy Madam Ritchie. She had just received the condolences of one of the eminent visitors. There was a somber air in the room and she led them to the room next door where Hope and Prudence, dressed in transparent nightgowns and similarly transparent dressing gowns, sat in soft armchairs — a picture of charming disconsolation. They wilted visibly when Detective-Sergeant Demosthenes H. de Goede entered and stood irresolutely between them.

He stuttered his questions excitedly, meaninglessly to everyone without the interpretation of his Meturgeman. Madam Ritchie was moved by the signs of consternation that she now noticed, for the second time, in the young man. She put her arm around his shoulder and led him to the third armchair. She nodded to her daughters to repeat the story for the umpteenth time. They told it in turn, supplementing one another continually, as they demonstrated the crime with eloquent movements of their bodies. Both Detective-Sergeant Demosthenes H. de Goede and Judge O'Hara were transported by

the picture of the young girls illuminating the outrage with
such discerning movements.

"That corresponds to the observations of Father R. from
Santorini," Judge O'Hara called out when they reached the
end of their tale. "That is eloquent witness to the fierce nature of the erotic vampire — the most lascivious of all *incubi*."

"And there's a love bite on her neck," whispered Madam
Richie.

Detective-Sergeant Demosthenes H. de Goede stuttered his
desire to see it, and thus to simplify for himself the task of dis-
tinguishing between the two, but Madam Ritchie put her hand
calmingly on his shoulder and gave him a small, soft, affec-
tionate squeeze.

She nodded to her daughters.

"It was a big man," said Prudence.

"His power was terrible," said Hope.

"One was powerless in his arms," said Prudence longingly.

"He was bigger and stronger than an ordinary person,"
said Hope carefully.

"Shortly after midnight," said Judge O'Hara, "the super-
natural appearance and disappearance, the mark on the left
side of the throat . . ." He suddenly stood up and pressed
his aspen staff to him. "It agrees perfectly with Slavonic tradi-
tions, and of a characteristic pattern."

Detective-Sergeant Demosthenes H. de Goede, too, stood
up. He stuttered his intention to leave no stone unturned,
he looked for the last time at the two pale girls with their
plaited hair hanging over their shoulders, their femininity so

vulnerably exposed. He repeated his intentions in a cold, measured stutter and left the room, purposeful in this final phase of his mission.

3

They reached the Welgevonden big house and rang the bell continuously until the Malay girl appeared, exposed her ruby smile and then asked them softly to follow her. She led them through all the rooms with all their treasures, which impeded their passage, to a small back room, on the door of which she knocked. That morning she wore a Malay dress, her eyes were kindly and friendly upon them.

Someone answered. She listened with an ear against the door, expanded her smile to the second ruby, opened the door and motioned to them to enter.

A moist heat beat up against Judge O'Hara and Detective-Sergeant Demosthenes H. de Goede. They could hardly recognize any objects for the mistiness that filled the room. But they gradually became accustomed to the dense atmosphere and then observed the "slim" Mrs. Silberstein naked in a *Lehmbad*, smeared up to her eyes with healing *mousse*. A *Badearzt* was busy massaging her body and was evidently dissatisfied over the compulsory interruption of his manipulations.

Detective-Sergeant Demosthenes H. de Goede stuttered as clearly as he could a single question: "Pffffft . . . ssssst . . . wrrrrrs . . . Adm . . . Kdm . . . Slbrsttttt?" and found, unexpectedly, understanding in the doctor who, with Teutonic thoroughness, described the exact position of the room.

They left the room before the "slim" Mrs. Silberstein could stop the attractive Sergeant, and followed the instructions until they reached a room that was locked. Judge O'Hara tapped on the door with his staff and called the name of Adam Kadmon Silberstein repeatedly, until Jock Silberstein appeared, unlocked the door and went ahead of them into an empty room.

"He has gone again," said Jock in amazement and looked anxiously out of the window.

4

They scoured all the well-known places on Welgevonden in their search. The inhabitants had not seen the Giant. One of the eminent visitors remembered clearly that he had seen the Giant but (thoughtfully with his finger to his temple) that had been the previous day at Mon Repos. Jock Silberstein left them to continue his search alone: he was already used to it; he spent most of his time these days looking for the Giant.

Now that Jock Silberstein was no longer present, the residents and relatives were much more outspoken. Everyone had heard of the second assault, on Hope . . . or was it Prudence? Lucky she had not suffered the fate of poor Lila.

"We loved Lila very much," said one of the residents, on his way to get a thiamine injection. "We loved Lila very much. We loved Lila very much."

An eminent visitor declared himself particularly interested in the methods of the Republic's C.I.D. and, with a bow to Judge O'Hara, the judiciary. Another visitor, attached to the press, was actively searching for the Giant, for an interview, and listened attentively to Judge O'Hara's dissertation on the erotic familiar or satyr that leeched onto his or her victim and drained his or her life force. He had his headline ready: VIRGINS OF WELGEVONDEN VICTIMS OF VOLUPTUOUS FAMILIAR.

Judge O'Hara informed Detective-Sergeant Demosthenes H. de Goede that Azazel, in the form of a corpse-devouring serpent, also exhibited the characteristics of the vampire — according to well-known authorities such as Kornmannus in his *Miraculus Mortuorum* and Paulus Schalichius in his treatise *De Demonio Infernali.* He added, however, that that doctrine was disputed by others, according to information in Carzov's *Disputatio de Gigantibus.* This was the first time Judge O'Hara had been accorded such interested attention and he enjoyed every moment of the search for the "pallid, blue-eyed, bloodsucking Giant," as he frequently called Adam Kadmon.

As the day progressed, it was as if the pattern of the search-for-retribution had taken hold of all the residents, relatives and guests as an ordinary acceptable fact about which there was no further discussion. Everyone was, in the meantime, very busy with the preparations for the ceremony that evening, and the rape of Lila-Hope-or-Prudence was a sideshow that added spice to the dish. Lila, the beloved daughter of the earlier pale-faced girl became, as the day passed, an example to everyone of the maiden taunted by the evil figure in his demoniacal mimicry. Hunt-the-Giant became an interlude in the preparations for the important ceremony.

Detective-Sergeant Demosthenes H. de Goede and Judge O'Hara came across the well-beloved Dries and his gamboling little bull on their way to the heifers' camp. Dries did not know where the Giant was, but had no doubt of the Giant's ultimate fate. He was happy as never before. The moment of recompense had arrived, his breeding policy had been worked out, the monster was destroyed — he exulted in the future matriarchy that he would humbly serve.

Everywhere there were tracks of the Giant: they found them at the fountain, the Scene of the Disaster. They found them all over the wet earth. They found them even at the little house with the asbestos roof where the uncle from Welkom and his family had opened the doors and shutters to the sunny day. They encouraged the Detective-Sergeant on his important search and waved to him from doors and windows.

They found Henry Silberstein-van Eeden engrossed with his own particular problem, unaware of what was happening.

They came across Professor Dreyer with a test tube in his hand, sequestered and isolated in his research room.

They found goodwill and encouragement everywhere. There was no one with misgivings; only a few who stood aloof. Detective-Sergeant Demosthenes H. de Goede relentlessly pursued his sole objective: the destruction of the monster, for the moment inaccessible.

5

At the cottage with all the notices, they saw the scrabbling figure of Dr. Johns behind the window. Detective-Sergeant Demosthenes H. de Goede took the key from Judge O'Hara and unlocked the door. The two decrepit old friends met and greeted one another in the passage as if nothing had happened.

Detective-Sergeant Demosthenes H. de Goede locked them both in and resumed his search.

There are certain times in one's life when one must complete one's task alone and outsiders are simply in the way. Detective-Sergeant Demosthenes H. de Goede's patience was exhausted. He was tired of trying in vain to distinguish between resident, guest and relative. It demanded certain sacrifices: he was without his Meturgeman and without the judge. Perhaps, later, there would be questions from the top, but he was ready to take the responsibility. There are moments which require decisions that only one can take.

He walked rapidly through the Foundation, from side to side. He saw all the preparations for the evening, the throng of helpers who were getting the hall in order, erecting the loudspeakers and putting up outside extensions. This was a search that he knew and was used to. The object had been determined; the time had now come for the object to be located. It was the final phase, the last, unavailing flight. The end was unavertable — he knew the form so well. There were even times in this phase that he pitied the fugitive. But he had learned at the police college that one had to extirpate that pity, roots and all.

6

Comparatively late in the day, around twelve o'clock, Detective-Sergeant Demosthenes H. de Goede found a naked figure with a long beard stretched out happily on the grass having a sunbath.

He arrested him at once and locked him in one of the glass rooms.

Once again he felt that feeling of sympathy, which he so often felt, but a rule was a rule. If one relented in regard to minor infringements, one weakened the principle. The function of pardoning belonged to the judge; the official's job was confined to his duty.

"It's not the persecutor who is without feeling," he wrote. "It's the one who lays down the laws. There must be certitude for the protection of the guilty as well as the innocent. Prosecution, punishment and prevention must be clearly distinguished and limited to their relevant departments. The police officer, the judge and sociologist has each his own separate function."

He picked up a fresh track of the Giant on the wet ground and looked attentively in the direction of the flat-trodden heather.

7

He came across a solitary girl at the fountain and recognized Hope. She wore her hair like a young girl, on either side of her shoulders. There was nobody else around. For a few wordless minutes they looked into each other's eyes and then she fell sobbing into his arms. She melted softly against his body and lifted her face to him. Her lips were moist and warm. She hung on his mouth, then pressed her face against his neck, and her teeth, in the fervent passion of her love, sank into his throat. He extricated himself with difficulty from her arms.

The Task had to be completed first. He stuttered a promise

for later in her ear. He would complete the Task for her —
and for her sister, the unfortunate resident.

He gave a last look back at her and resumed his search, as
the day passed and the preparations approached their completion.

8

He wrote: "Welgevonden is a beautiful place. It's a true Paradise. Who am I, unworthy human being, that I presume to
regain Paradise for them and for my loved one?"

He sat with his back to one of the masks and looked lazily
in the midday sun at the sun's rays playing on the water. He
stroked the place where she bit him and then he stood up lan-
guorously and resumed his wandering. The setter, Fido, appeared from behind a bush. Detective-Sergeant Demosthenes
H. de Goede turned to stone. He looked around carefully.

The trees swayed in the wind, the lawn was empty and there
was no sign of anyone.

9

The sun had set and Detective-Sergeant Demosthenes H. de
Goede returned to his room to change for the evening. He
shaved, bathed and dressed in a tuxedo. The lights had come
on and residents, relatives and guests were already on their
way to the hall; the noise they made came from all sides.

But there was still much time. His jacket hung over the
chair and he lay stretched out on his bed, his hands folded behind his head, watching the woman from Sweden who was
putting on the most beautiful lace underclothing and stand-

ing before the mirror doing her makeup, before getting into a golden evening dress.

He longed suddenly for Hope and then he began to dream of a little house in one of the suburbs. It was the night of the Police Ball, in aid of the Orphans' Fund. She, too, would make herself beautiful for him before a mirror: the attractive wife of Lieutenant Demosthenes H. de Goede.

He smiled all of a sudden and wrote, lying on his back: "It's not dreams that estrange one from reality; it's reality that estranges one from one's dreams."

Then he stood up. The time had come. First he took his weapon from the little trunk, turned it rapidly around his forefinger and placed it carefully in the holster strapped around his shoulder. Then he put on his jacket leisurely and stuck the *ephialtion* in his buttonhole.

The lights in the Swedish woman's glass house had gone out some time before, and she stood there, wide-eyed, in the dark watching him arming himself. Then he, too, switched out the light and walked slowly past the house, in which she hid herself in terror, toward the hall, to be in time for the ceremony.

10

The hall was crammed. The lights shone through the windows and the glass doors onto the grass, and still the people came. On the platform was a row of chairs on which the dignitaries would sit and, slightly to one side, the chairs for the rector and for those who would receive the honorary degrees. There were gladioli in a vase on a little table and there were portraits of the Founders on the walls. This was the hall in which the residents and their families gathered every morning, for prayers and to receive their instructions for the day. The front half was filled with residents and their relatives, who turned around continually to stare at the guests who occupied the back seats. Whenever one of the dignitaries entered the hall and was led by a guide to the platform, a ripple of talk passed through the crowd and the identity of the new arrival was excitedly discussed.

The other residents, relatives and guests, who could not find seats inside, sat outside on the grass or stood around in groups. It was a lovely evening: not too cold, not too hot, and the masks droned monotonously in the distance.

At a certain time a small group of inhabitants mounted the platform in single file and produced a violin, a saw and an accordion. They started off at once with "Bootjie na Kammaland" and followed that with "Siembamba, Mamma se Kindjie."

There was great applause when Jock Silberstein and "slim" Mrs. Silberstein appeared and took their places on the platform. The cheering was repeated when Henry Silberstein-van Eeden followed soon afterward. One chair still remained empty and they all kept their eyes on that. The well-beloved Dries appeared on the platform, a mourning band around his arm, and the audience rose to their feet as one man. They all sat down again with a shuffling of chairs when Dries made a slight bow and took his place on the empty chair. Then they renewed their cheering when the rector of a well-known university appeared, followed by other high dignitaries, and

took up the remaining chairs. Here and there someone offered a chair to a lady, and one or two extra were passed from
the back of the hall and placed on the platform.

The orchestra, composed of residents, ended the song with
". . . chuck him in the ditch, stamp on his head and he'll be
dead," and left the platform in file, grinning broadly at the
other residents, who whistled, stamped on the floor and
bawled for an encore. A guide prevented the orchestra from
returning to the platform.

Detective-Sergeant Demosthenes H. de Goede had just arrived and peeped into the hall. Then he disappeared unnoticed
among the people on the grass and reconnoitered the surroundings.

The master of ceremonies, in a dinner jacket, had just begun
speaking, welcoming the rector and introducing certain of the
best-known dignitaries to the audience. An unpretentious little program by residents and relatives would be completed
before the actual performance started. Small locusts in black
stockings streamed onto the platform, joined in a solid black
mass and, their eyes fixed on landscapes by weekend painters
on the walls, filled the hall with the ominous sounds of a children's voice choir: loudspeakers carried the sounds outside
where the swelling crowd listened in dead silence to the disembodied little voices. The little white faces of the locusts
whispered a last speculation on death and then the ranks disintegrated, to thunderous cheers, especially from their relatives.

The change was quick and testified to strict discipline. The
heavy piano was swiftly moved by a crowd of tots and the

next moment, the voices, with accompaniment, echoed through the hall to the outside, where the multitude sat back to back looking at the far horizon where a red glow from Mon Repos lit the landscape beautifully.

Occasionally someone sang a solo; occasionally there was a duet. Then the residents' orchestra was recalled for the finale: the lugubrious saw, the free-ranging violin, the ululating accordion, as the choir finally repeated: "Siembamba, mama's pet, chuck him in the ditch; stamp on his head and he'll be d-e-a-d!"

11

And still they came, singly and in pairs, to find a place on the grass. Also a giant figure who had seen the lights from afar and heard the songs and who smiled like a child at the familiar tune.

He came soundlessly nearer through the trees and suddenly stopped at a small building. It was the place where the day before he had heard the drone and seen the mist. There was nobody around and he entered the little room. When he switched on the light he saw the coiled pipes against the wall and the two big taps. He opened both taps simultaneously and listened attentively to the increasing sound, as the steam enveloped him. The roaring grew louder, the light grew dim and he was alone in a white world. His mouth opened and shut and he was aware of himself screaming something in the ghostly mist. But he understood nothing. His mind groped in vain for the words that he could not hear. Something inside him was absolutely still, soundless. In the room of con-

fession he had found words but, alas, no thoughts. It was only
the sound that thundered on endlessly around him, and he accepted the sounds as he accepted all the sounds all around him
every day. He felt wet and clammy and was invaded by lassitude. He leaned against the wall and felt the taps against
his back. He felt for them and turned them off. Suddenly the
noise stopped, and the mist dispersed gradually. He repeated
the game until he was bored and then he left the little room —
drawn like a moth to the lights and the other noise in the distance.

12

The master of ceremonies had just introduced a well-known
professor, who would read Jock Silberstein's *curriculum vitae*.

He spoke of the achievements of that dynamic man, who
had first made his mark in the farming-industrial sphere
when, in the twilight of his life, he had used his material wealth
to bring clarity into the shadowed lives of the multitude. In a
community in which the formula had replaced the myth, he
was perhaps in the process of transforming formula to myth.
In this Foundation of his he was, for inhabitant and member
of the family, clothing the commonplace in the raiment of
fabulous significance. Perhaps his methods were unconven-
tional; perhaps it was in conflict with present-day *procédé*,
but in his attempt to restore continuity he brought, in his own
manner, light into the darkness of troubled minds that needed
light so much.

The speaker peered over the uplifted faces in the direction
of the darkness outside.

Perhaps it had been granted him to restore the interlude on a plane where experience would replace decadent repetition; where the symbol would replace the sign; where logic would find coexistence in the boldest flight of the imagination . . .

As he spoke, Jock Silberstein looked, too, at the darkness outside. But his attention was far removed from the speaker. He had looked in vain among the faces in the hall and was searching now — where he could distinguish moving figures in the light on the grass — for a single, giant figure outside.

The Giant had appeared at the edge of the light. He heard the voice from the loudspeaker, he looked at the gathering and he was filled with an irresistible desire to join them, too. He tugged nervously at the scarlet ribbon around his neck and walked carefully nearer.

Jock Silberstein had just received cap and gown. He bowed to the guests as a Doctor, *honoris causa*, and he smiled acknowledgment of the thunderous applause with the aloof reserve of someone who has long since escaped from the clutches of self-assertion.

The master of ceremonies waited for him to take his seat next to the beaming Mrs. Silberstein, and then he raised his hand for silence. Another eminent official of the university was called upon to read the *curriculum vitae* of Henry Silberstein-van Eeden. Soon after he started speaking the Giant appeared in the full light on the lawn.

The people in the hall, intent on the words of the speaker, were unaware of what was happening outside. They did not hear the stifled cries of the women, they did not see the men who, prompted by their strength in numbers, took up a threatening position. As the Giant, protected by that insensitivity

born of his retarded mentality, reached the middle of the
lawn, the crowd formed into a strong, growing circle around
him. The gathering became as strong as the Giant himself; it
became, as a mass, the equal of the Giant — a source of power
that would measure power against power. The single rational
cohesion disappeared; the single fear became the fear of everyone; reason disappeared in the throng; a primeval urge appeared to combat a primordial phenomenon. The huge figure
carried the banner of evil, the scarlet ribbon of demoniacal
powers; the dense throng carried the white banner of the
crushed virgin. The troubled complexity of their lives was
reduced to a simple truth. All the unintelligible conflicts
within them suddenly assumed the appearance of understandable simplicity. By means of the alchemy of their mass
thought-process the whore became a virgin and the nymphomaniac a threatened nymph. In their collective simplicity
they knew only a dichotomy. The whole complexity of life
became understandable through their mass action. They were
filled with a sense of wonderful freedom, faced with the joy of
an easy choice. The first stone that sailed through the air for
the sake of Lila freed them from the bondage inherent in themselves. Every stone and every fling was a further step to lib-
eration: the atavism that characterized the act was a progres-
sion that stimulated reason. Egged on by the promise, stupefied by their fury, they threw one stone after another at the
easy target.

At first the Giant, thinking it a game, threw the stones back.
One struck a woman on the mouth and she collapsed, blood
flowing, which, appearing black in the electric light, left the

impression of lungs crushed. The crowd droned nearer and threw the stones like hunters: the act was released from its greater meaning and brought down to a basis of maximum effectiveness. Many young men doubled themselves up to give a whiplash to their throws and to get, for the sake of the admiration of many young women, the stone into the target bull. It became a carnival — with the masks roaring and under the colored glare from Mon Repos. It was a Coney Island of the spirit — while the lecture continued over the loudspeaker. There were screams, there were lights and noise, there was the challenge of pretty eyes and the promise of reward for success. Even an eminent guest, from a lesser country, conscious of the ability of his forefathers and homesick for his native land, threw a stone at the target and struck the bull, to the loud applause of a female guest, relatives and residents.

And there, still, was the Giant, with no apprehension of the nature of events. The stones hurt him, but he was strong and his threshold of pain was high. There was on his face a smile of pure joy, he bared his sharp teeth as a wonderful feeling overpowered him: it was the first time he had been accepted by everyone, that they had wanted to play with him. Sometimes his smile changed to a grimace of pain when a stone struck him squarely on the body or the head, but then his face beamed again with pleasure. He was unaware of the blood that began flowing from his temples, and of the swollen bruises that began to form where the tissue was injured. He was unaware that, with every injury, his appearance grew uglier and more grotesque. He returned stone for stone in this strange and interesting game.

When, here and there, a stone hit someone — even when the throwers missed the Giant and struck one another — it was as if the crowd's fury mounted to a new level. The uglier the Giant grew under systematic injury, the more passionate the crowd became. They had now reached the stage at which they had developed beyond their feeling of self-justification and beyond their hunter's instinct. When a chance stone struck a young girl, an extraordinary quavering sound rose from the mob. They approached murderously, but they did not yet dare to lay a hand on the Giant.

While all this was happening outside, the voice of the speaker came clear and strong over the microphone. The voice spoke of the zeal with which Henry Silberstein-van Eeden served the Foundation. He described the work done there. He dealt with the concept of moral responsibility and he warned against the confusion in our use of ethical concepts, the illogical use of words that did not distinguish between the attribution of blame and a qualitative judgment of a situation. On a place like the Foundation, where the basis of moral responsibility was restricted to the minimum, one came nearest to a tragic situation. And it was on this terrain that someone like Henry Silberstein-van Eeden performed his difficult work.

He too, like the previous speaker, looked to the darkness behind the lights outside, completely unaware, like everyone in the hall, of what was happening there. He described the unbearable feeling of disintegration without the possibility of casting blame; the fear in the wake of destruction by an object of destiny which is beyond one's reach. And perhaps it was Henry's task, in this work he was doing, to make clearer the meaning of the scapegoat; to enable everyone, indeed all the inhabitants of this weary planet, to conquer in the shrinking world of individual responsibility his solitude and defenselessness by means of an exalted accusation.

As he spoke, Henry looked outside. He, too, saw nothing, but deep within him he had a feeling that somewhere something infinitely important was happening. It was difficult to describe because it was a concept that he could not formulate. It was as if he were finding a sort of reconciliation with the Foundation and as if Salome were living again for him. There were tears in his eyes while the sacrifice outside was taking place — without his knowledge, but in an extraordinary way his own responsibility.

While cap and gown were being donned and the crowd cheered deafeningly, Detective-Sergeant Demosthenes H. de Goede appeared on the scene and prepared himself to defend the threatened people. The Giant had only now begun to detect the animosity of the crowd and he staggered around, stunned, as the stones, hitting him where they had struck before, really hurt him. He was no longer a big child joining in the game, but a lost child overwhelmed by an incomprehensible anxiety. And, like a child, he began crying softly. The tears rolled down his cheeks and he grimaced crookedly with grief. His hands were raised and he struggled around helplessly, moaning with that lowing sound peculiar to the mentally retarded. When one of the men dared to approach close to him and hit him on the head with a stick, he brushed him to the ground, unconscious, with a single movement of his hand.

Detective-Sergeant Demosthenes H. de Goede's duty was plain. He jumped forward athletically and chopped a karate blow on his neck, jerking his head up and making him grunt with pain. Then Detective-Sergeant Demosthenes H. de Goede leaped back, out of reach of the flailing arms.

The Giant now wept aloud like a wounded child, but the multitude heard it as a roar of fury. The soft figures of Hope and Prudence (their hair combed out over their shoulders) pressed for protection against Detective-Sergeant Demosthenes H. de Goede.

Taking advantage of the Giant's bewildered condition, someone gashed him with a stone over the eye. The Giant spun around and searched, half blindly, with grasping hands, for his attacker. Detective-Sergeant Demosthenes H. de Goede was like lightning and struck him with a perfect bolo-hit in the other eye. He danced lightly away to where Hope and Prudence were waiting for him.

The Giant was now completely blinded by the blood in his eyes. The blood mingled with the tears, and dribbled on the corners of his mouth. He was sobbing so hard that he could scarcely breathe; he was so confused that he could not escape. The mob came carefully nearer. It was not so easy to finish off a Giant: it demanded time and determination. A courageous woman struck him on the body with a stick, but was hit by one of his arms. She rolled across the grass in a flowered line. Detective-Sergeant Demosthenes H. de Goede was, however, at hand, and delivered a swift and perfect ostrich kick straight to the Giant's stomach. He followed that up with a full nelson, but had to get out of the way quickly as even his muscular arms were wrenched loose. Two of the little darts the Giant had found at Mon Repos fell from his pocket, as well as a few marbles and a catapult. The crowd growled when it saw them. Someone jumped forward and picked up the two darts. He threw quickly. One missed and one struck the Giant near an eye. The Giant raised a hand to his face, withdrew the arrow and flung it away with a clumsy gesture. Detective-Sergeant Demosthenes H. de Goede deflected it with his arm, retrieved it and threw it skillfully back. The crowd cheered when it struck the Giant near his other eye.

And then, as if the possibility of flight had dawned on him, the Giant began to move slowly toward the darkness. Detective-Sergeant Demosthenes H. de Goede was quick to bar his way. He stood directly in the Giant's path, one foot forward, Hope's shawl in both hands. He waited until the stumbling Giant was upon him, and then executed a perfect veronica. As the Giant staggered past him, he punched him neatly behind the ear, giving the Giant momentum and making him fall over his feet.

Detective-Sergeant Demosthenes H. de Goede was dead calm. He stood waiting elegantly, a neat figure in his dress shirt and tuxedo. With a suspicion of vanity, perhaps, he raised a hand to his lapel, bent it around and smelled the *ephialtion*. The crowd had fallen silent and was looking at the Giant lying on the ground. The sobs had abated, the big face was swollen, the red hair damp, tousled and caked. And then the big figure began to rise, grunting and groaning as if even those enormous, clumsy legs could no longer carry the body. The Giant's hands hung at his sides, his neck was crooked, his back bent. He had stopped crying. He turned his back slowly and painfully on the people and began, slowly at first and then more quickly, to stumble away toward the waters roaring in the dark.

Detective-Sergeant Demosthenes H. de Goede took his Beretta .35 slowly from its holster, while the crowd grew quite quiet again. In a loud voice he ordered Adam Kadmon Silberstein three times to stop and then he aimed with his right arm out straight and his left hand on his hip. He aimed low deliberately, to conform to police regulations, and then fired. The report was dulled by the renewed cheering as the well-beloved Dries rose to his feet to expound the life, struggle and death of Uncle Giepie. Everyone saw the Giant stumble for a moment, stop and then disappear into the dark with a dragging foot.

It was all over. He would not get far. Detective-Sergeant Demosthenes H. de Goede replaced the weapon carefully and received embraces from Hope and Prudence with calm self-control. He was surrounded by the crowd and lifted on their shoulders, but he remained a model of modesty. He gazed thoughtfully at the jubilant residents, relatives and guests. It was as if a song of praise were arising. He thought of the words of Dr. Johns. Order had been restored.

After everyone had calmed down and left him free to complete his task, he looked at Hope and Prudence, who were laughing with complete abandon, and then confirmed his

choice. He took the *ephialtion* from his buttonhole and offered it to Hope, who blushed charmingly and received the
pledge shyly from her lover. The task was accomplished;
the drama ended. In the distance, against the horizon, the
fires of the Mon Repos churches burned a fiery red. And he
walked slowly toward the glow to complete his assignment.

QUANDO?

QUANDO? · 1 · In the penumbra
between the lights of the hall and the
lights of Mon Repos the monster struggled
with his shattered leg. He reached the first mask
that roared, and clung to it with his mighty arms. In the
twilight world of his thoughts there was no light. He was
filled with an irresistible longing for the one he loved, but he
did not know where to find him. From force of habit he
lowered himself into the stream, but nothing warned him
that his powers were exhausted. Even when the stream tore
him away from the mask and the waters roared in his face, he
was not aware of what was happening to him. As he floun-
dered in vain and disappeared under the stream, he was still
fighting against things he did not understand.

Deafening cheers came from the lighted hall and the Giant
began his last journey upon the noisy stream. The crowd had
risen to sing the song of the Foundation at the pitch of their
voices, and the second mask spat the heavy object from its
raging maw. The proceedings were concluded with three
loud hurrahs for the alumni and the third mask rattled and
struggled to rid itself of the object in its throat. The residents,
relatives and eminent guests were amiably on their way to
their glass houses when the fourth mask vomited the monster.
The lights were already out when the so-manyeth mask fell
dumb and then resumed all of a sudden its threnody. Only the
isolated flashes from the searching detective shone like a
lost firefly in the surroundings, as one mask after another
wrestled with the object that grew larger and larger. The
wind had already blown the plastic swan across the grass, lay-

ing as track a swollen counterpart. The Giant of Welgevonden was slowly but surely on his way to his final appointment, with a setter in a lily pond.

2

It was midnight and the moon shone over the Foundation. But
many were not asleep. The windows were open and Dr.
Johns, Judge O'Hara, Jock Silberstein, Henry Silberstein-
van Eeden and many guests and residents lay looking at the
phosphorescent orb among the tattered clouds. The light
shone down and was reflected from their faces: it brightened
the countenance of a living-dead, the white incisors grinning
in caves and towers. Hope and Prudence rolled around restlessly in their beds. The wind keened through the trees. But
the monster was satisfied. There was peace at Welgevonden.
The monster lay on his back, swollen and satisfied with life-
giving blood, his eyes fixed blindly on the moon.

3

The cellar thundered under the destructive assault to drive
out the evil spirits; the noise repeated the masks' cry of fear;
it tried in vain to extirpate the question in the heart of the
Founder; it was as meaningless as the stuttering sounds from
the hero at the door. The Giant of Welgevonden lay on a table in the cellar with his hands folded to form the unmentionable Name of God. The scarlet ribbon around his neck
had been washed pure white by the waters.

And then, when the first light of the rising sun shone on the

windows, the noise suddenly ceased, and in the silence that followed a song rose in the morning air: the "Adon 'Olam" in
praise of God as the eternal Ruler of the incomprehensible
Universe.

It was a song of praise, incomparably beautiful, for the dead,
the goat of God and the goat of the wilderness.